Road Trips Can Be Murder

Connie Shelton

Books by Connie Shelton

THE CHARLIE PARKER MYSTERY SERIES

Deadly Gamble
Vacations Can Be Murder
Partnerships Can Be Murder
Small Towns Can Be Murder
Memories Can Be Murder
Honeymoons Can Be Murder
Reunions Can Be Murder
Competition Can Be Murder
Balloons Can Be Murder
Obsessions Can Be Murder
Gossip Can Be Murder
Stardom Can Be Murder
Phantoms Can Be Murder
Buried Secrets Can Be Murder
Legends Can Be Murder
Weddings Can Be Murder
Alibis Can Be Murder
Escapes Can Be Murder
Sweethearts Can Be Murder
Money Can Be Murder
Road Trips Can Be Murder
Holidays Can Be Murder - a Christmas novella

THE SAMANTHA SWEET SERIES

Sweet Masterpiece
Sweet's Sweets
Sweet Holidays
Sweet Hearts
Bitter Sweet
Sweets Galore
Sweets, Begorra
Sweet Payback
Sweet Somethings
Sweets Forgotten
Spooky Sweet
Sticky Sweet
Sweet Magic
Deadly Sweet Dreams
The Ghost of Christmas Sweet
Tricky Sweet
Spellbound Sweets - a Halloween novella
The Woodcarver's Secret

THE HEIST LADIES SERIES

Diamonds Aren't Forever
The Trophy Wife Exchange
Movie Mogul Mama
Homeless in Heaven
Show Me the Money

CHILDREN'S BOOKS

Daisy and Maisie and the Great Lizard Hunt
Daisy and Maisie and the Lost Kitten

Road Trips
Can Be
Murder

Charlie Parker Mysteries, Book 21

Connie Shelton

Secret Staircase Books

Road Trips Can Be Murder
Published by Secret Staircase Books, an imprint of
Columbine Publishing Group, LLC
PO Box 416, Angel Fire, NM 87710

Book layout and design by Secret Staircase Books
Cover images © Konstantin Sutyagin, Frank Armstrong, Gregory21
First trade paperback edition: March, 2023
First e-book edition: March, 2023
* * *

Publisher's Cataloging-in-Publication Data

Shelton, Connie
Road Trips Can Be Murder / by Connie Shelton.
p. cm.
ISBN 978-1649141248 (paperback)
ISBN 978-1649141255 (e-book)

1. Charlie Parker (Fictitious character)—Fiction. 2. New Mexico—Fiction. 3. Arizona—Fiction. 4. Con artists—Fiction. 5. Women sleuths—Fiction. I. Title

Charlie Parker Mystery Series : Book 21.
Shelton, Connie, Charlie Parker mysteries.

BISAC : FICTION / Mystery & Detective.

813/.54

For Dan who keeps our household running while I'm buried in the lives of my characters and their tricky situations
and

To you, my readers. You make it all worthwhile.

Chapter 1

You know the kind of day that starts out with all kinds of promise, the one where you're having a leisurely second coffee over breakfast, and the only other thing on the schedule is to get a pedicure and then come home to read a novel? The Thursday before Thanksgiving started out like that for me. Then the perfect plan completely tanked. There was no way I could have foreseen a grueling drive with a couple of unwanted passengers and a missing-person investigation before the weekend was out.

Hang on—I'm about to share the whole grisly tale.

It began when I strolled into my office at RJP Investigations and heard Ron's voice call out to me from across the hall.

"Charlie, before you get comfortable …"

I hadn't actually planned on staying long enough to get comfortable. I only meant to pop in to pick up the aforementioned novel, which I'd (stupidly) left behind after my trip to the bookstore yesterday afternoon. But now I was caught. My brother's voice held the tone that told me he was about to dump some extra work on me.

Very deliberately, I left my shoulder bag in place and held the keys to my Jeep in hand, so he'd get the idea. Didn't happen.

"We've got a new assignment," he said, pawing through several layers of the clutter on his desk.

I picked up on the word. He didn't say it was a new case. Silly me, I bit.

"Assignment?"

"Yeah, it's not really an investigation. Just a quick road trip."

My second mistake was letting the faint flicker of interest show in my expression. I do love a fun bit of travel now and then.

"Good—I knew you'd be perfect for it," he said, handing over a slip of paper with his familiar scrawl on it.

I recognized the name of a street in Santa Fe. There was an address and a name. "So it involves driving to Santa Fe and back?"

"Partially."

That's when my alarm bells should have begun screaming, but I supposed I could drive up there after my pedicure, which I was due for in an hour's time. "Okay, so what does that mean, and why aren't you doing it?"

He stood up, circled his desk, and reached for his Stetson on the rack near his door. "I've got court. The case where we investigated the background on that woman who bilked her boyfriend's estate of a hundred thousand dollars. It's hitting Judge Walter's courtroom this morning and I'm subpoenaed to testify."

"Okay, I get it. Court cannot be ignored. But what's so important in Santa Fe that it must be done today?"

"Walk with me down to my car," he said, pushing past me in the hall.

I trailed along. "And what did you mean when you said *partially*? What on earth is this new assignment?"

We descended the staircase of the old Victorian where our office operates. Sally, our part-time receptionist, sat at her desk and tapped away at her keyboard. She didn't really meet my eyes, just gave a quick wave and went back to her work.

Through the kitchen at the back of the building, Ron kept talking. "So, there's this kid. A girl who needs to be delivered to her mother. Social Services picked her up."

"And this became our job because …?"

"Because it's a road trip. They don't have anyone who can break away—understaffed, and all that. The police have definite jurisdictional boundaries, so they've hired us to do it."

"Seriously. Isn't that what Uber is for?"

Ron had opened the back door and stepped back to allow me to walk ahead. "The girl is a runaway. She's being returned to her custodial parent. It's more complicated than an Uber driver can handle. Plus, it would be a helluva lot more expensive."

I stopped in my tracks. "Exactly how far away does the kid's mother live?"

He shuffled a little uncomfortably. "Uh, Phoenix."

"Okay, wait. I need to drive to Santa Fe, pick up this girl from Social Services, and then drive her all the way to Phoenix? That's a minimum of eight or nine hours of driving."

He sent me The Look. "For you, Miss Leadfoot, I'm sure you can accomplish it in seven. Get started now, and you'll have her there by dinner time tonight. Get yourself a room somewhere and enjoy a leisurely drive home by yourself tomorrow."

He glanced at the book in my hand. "Think of it—a quiet evening in a hotel to read all you want, and then you'll have two days free to bake pies with Elsa. I promise. No work over the weekend."

I had to admit, that held a certain appeal. I cannot tell you how many times a case has become a 24/7 proposition. "Trade cars with me."

He eyed his sporty Mustang parked next to my Jeep. The Wrangler is perfect as my around-town vehicle and great for Drake's and my getaways to the mountains, but as a long-haul interstate highway vehicle its comfort leaves something to be desired. I could make the trip in less time and with less hip-agony, and he realized I would be a much happier camper that way.

"Okay." He grumbled a little and held out his keys. "You take care of it and mind your speed."

"You watch my baby in those parking garages downtown," I reminded.

"Deal." He reached into the slender portfolio he'd carried downstairs and pulled out two sheets of paper. "Here are your details and the authorization form from the caseworker for you to take custody of the girl."

I glanced over it and took in the particulars. Pick up one

Sophie Marie O'Connell at the Health and Social Services building in Santa Fe, and deliver her to Dixie O'Connell in Mesa, Arizona. The delivery address was on Brown Road, which I knew from previous visits to Mesa to be a major street, so I hoped the drop-off would be as quick and simple as Ron had hinted. Sophie was thirteen years old, thankfully not a little child. We could probably fill the time with girl talk and it would pass quickly.

I figured one hour to Santa Fe, a few minutes to pick up the girl and sign the release form, another hour back to Albuquerque. I wouldn't even bother with an overnight bag. This time of year I carry an emergency kit in the Jeep—a heavy coat, snow boots, insulated water bottle, and a supply of power bars and energy snacks. It's my just-in-case for the times we make last-minute plans to go to our little mountain cabin or take a day for snowshoeing. Not that there's enough snow in mid-November to really count. While Ron transferred my bag to the trunk of his car I called and cancelled my pedicure.

Sitting in the Mustang, I took a minute to get familiar with the buttons and dials, and I checked the weather forecast on my phone. Everything looked clear and good.

Little did I know.

Chapter 2

Exactly fifty-four minutes later I pulled into the parking lot at my Santa Fe destination. I didn't know the layout of the government building, but a helpful directory of white letters on a black background sent me to Room 207. Elena Garcia awaited my arrival and looked somewhat relieved that I had arrived before her lunch break. She tilted her head toward a glassed-in room where I saw a teen sitting at a Formica-topped table, her eyes intent on her phone, thumbs moving a mile a minute.

"That's Sophie," Elena told me. She had already picked up a manila folder and was on her way to the room where Sophie waited.

She didn't look up when we entered. I noted a slender young woman with lithe limbs, wearing a short white flared skirt, bolero length red jacket with fringe down the front, and red cowboy boots. Her blonde hair hung straight to the middle of her back and shielded her face, but I spotted a soft jawline and straight nose.

"Sophie? Your ride is here," Elena said.

No reaction.

Elena crossed to the far side of the room and lifted a backpack that sat on the floor. "Don't forget your things." She plopped it on the table, inches from the girl's phone.

"Okay, I *get* it," Sophie said. After a full minute she took her eyes from the phone and looked at us, revealing dark brown eyes and a deep dimple in her chin. She wore minimal makeup and seemed somehow self-conscious about that.

"Hi, Sophie. I'm Charlie. Looks like I'll be driving you to your mom's house today."

The girl grunted something unintelligible and turned her back to me as she hefted the backpack over one shoulder. Her phone pinged with a message, and her eyes went there instantly.

Elena and I exchanged a look. She held up the manila folder and pulled out a sheet for me to sign, basically a receipt for the kid. My copy of the page contained the address I'd be heading for, along with the mother's name and a contact number for her. We walked out into the hall.

"So, tell me what else I need to know about my young charge. Is she going to take off the minute I go to the restroom?"

"No, I don't think so. She's been on the streets for a couple months, and she seems willing enough to go back to her mom. As long as you aren't expecting sparkling conversation from her, you'll do fine."

"Yeah, I kind of got that already." I glanced again at the printed sheet in my hand. "Anything else I need to know? Hot-button topics to stay away from?"

Elena shook her head. "You'll be fine."

"I basically have zero experience with kids, just so you know."

She glanced toward the windowed room. Sophie emerged a second later. "It's just a one-day drive. Everything will be fine. Mrs. O'Connell is expecting you."

And with that we were on the way out to the parking lot. Sophie seemed mildly impressed with the Mustang. Well, okay, I'm only guessing that by the fact that she actually looked at the car instead of at her phone as I unlocked the doors and then stashed her pack in the trunk.

A chill wind whipped through the lot, lifting the girl's short skirt. November is a capricious month here in our region. Santa Fe sits at 7,000 feet and there had already been snowfall on the nearby ski slopes. I considered asking Sophie if she had something warmer to change into, but discarded the idea as she continued to ignore me. We'd be in the car for the rest of the day and into a warmer climate by evening.

"We'll gas up here, and that ought to get us most of the way down the road," I said, starting the engine. "Have you had lunch yet? Want something?"

"I'm good." It was the first time I'd heard her actually speak, as she hadn't even said goodbye to Elena or acknowledged the woman's help. Good to know she could talk.

I steered toward a station I'm familiar with on the south end of the city, where I topped up the tank and went inside for a selection of snacks. Twenty minutes later we were on I-25 again. Within a few miles, traffic had slowed to a crawl. And then my phone rang.

Drake's name appeared on the screen and I went to hands-free mode.

"Hon, do you still have the spare key for my truck? I'm locked out."

"Um …" Keys had been the furthest subject from my mind at that moment as I stuffed two Cheetos into my mouth. "Pretty sure I do."

"Are you anywhere close enough to drop them off to me here at Double Eagle?"

The airport where he hangars his helicopter was close to ninety minutes away at this point, and I told him that. I'd already texted him about my little road trip. I fished around in the side pocket of my purse, on the floor behind the passenger seat, and there I felt the familiar shape of his key fob.

"I'll love you forever if you can detour long enough to bring them by."

I laughed. "You'll love me forever anyway. And part of the reason is because I always carry spare keys for you. As soon as I can get out of this construction zone on La Bajada, I'll break the sound barrier to get to you."

"Don't take chances. I've got plenty of maintenance I can do here to kill some time."

By the time we ended the call, Sophie was eyeing me with mild curiosity. I held out the Cheetos bag but she shook her head.

"I guess you heard. We need to make an extra stop." I glanced over to see her shrug and go back to her phone screen, ignoring the Cheetos.

As traffic inched along at less than twenty miles an hour, I peeked sideways long enough to figure out she was scrolling endlessly through short videos on TikTok.

My attention went quickly back to the vehicles around me, and I saw that the construction barriers ended about a half-mile in the distance. By the time the road widened again with both lanes fully open, all the aggression in about eighty drivers opened up too. Pickup trucks vied with sleek sports cars to see who could get to the head of the line, as if there really was a first place in this silly race.

Part of me wanted to take advantage of the Mustang's power and roar ahead, but I didn't. The day was already not going according to my original plan. No point in bringing myself to the boiling point. I held it to the speed limit and let the others battle it out until there was at least a mile or two clear ahead of me. Then I let the sporty car have its way.

I found myself wondering about my passenger. What was Sophie's story? But when I tried conversation, she simply gave me a disdainful look. "Can't you see that I'm busy?"

I wanted to retort with, "Can't *you* see that you're rude?" My mouth opened and then shut again. I would be the bigger person. Mentally, I began ticking off the remaining hours in this stupid trip until I could drop her off and let her mother deal with her.

We caught up with the same set of aggressive trucks and cars as we approached the outskirts of Albuquerque, and I realized it was now well into the lunch hour. This means everyone in town has decided to eat out, and most will choose a place clear across town from their work. Or they're all racing toward Costco to stock up on supplies for the upcoming holiday week. I-25 was in full kill-or-be-killed mode. I concentrated on nothing more than getting through it, onto westbound I-40, and reaching the exit for the small westside airport where Drake would be waiting.

I dictated a short text: I'm here. Meet me at the gate.

And he did. I got out of the car and shook out the tension in my shoulders.

"How's it going?" he asked, pulling me into a hug.

I think I just rolled my eyes, but the hug felt great. I dug into the purse for his keys. "Freckles is at Gram's. I know she and Dottie would keep her overnight, but maybe it's better if you pick her up when you get home. She'll be eager for a walk to the park."

"Let me know when you get settled in your hotel," he said. "And be careful."

I touched the smidge of gray at his temples. For a guy in his late forties, he can be amazingly old-fashioned. But I loved the caring attention he always showed me.

"Will do. And when I get back tomorrow we'll grab enchiladas at Pedro's."

"Absolutely. All my flights tomorrow are local." He stepped closer for a kiss and I could sense Sophie's eyes on us. *So what?*

"Well, I'd better get going."

"Watch the weather. There's a front moving in, but as long as you get south of the Mogollon Rim before midnight you should be okay."

The Rim, I knew from previous jobs with him, was the geological feature that divided Arizona's high desert to the north from the lower Sonoran Desert in the southern part of the state. The quick drop of four thousand feet in elevation meant the difference between snow or rain, cloudy or clear, an easy trip or a rough one, as one traversed the state. With only six more hours to our destination, we should be fine.

Two hours into it, just beyond Gallup, a packing crate fell off the back of an eighteen- wheeler, shattered, and came at me so suddenly that I couldn't avoid hitting one of the boards. I hoped for the best, but a few seconds later I felt the telltale bump and tug of a flat tire.

Great. Just great.

Chapter 3

I steered carefully to the edge, as far off the road as I could get. There wasn't a rest area or an exit in sight. Well, okay. This is what roadside assistance is for. I reached behind my seat for my purse and yanked out my wallet. Sophie had dropped her phone into her lap and was actually looking at me instead. For once.

"It'll be fine. We've got good insurance and this'll be no big deal to them." I dialed the toll-free number on the back of my insurance card.

"Thank you for calling roadside assistance. If someone in your vehicle is injured, please hang up and call 9-1-1 immediately. For mechanical breakdowns, press 1."

I complied.

"Welcome to your roadside assistance directory. Please be advised that our call volume is currently higher than normal. Your wait time

for an associate to answer is estimated to be fifty-five minutes."

Well, crud. I could certainly change the tire myself in less time than that. Especially considering that was just the time it would take to get someone on the phone. It could easily be another hour before a truck would actually arrive.

I put on the emergency blinkers, cautiously opened my door, and stepped out to assess the situation. Luckily, the flat was on the right side of the car, away from the traffic that continued to roar past at eighty miles an hour. I debated getting back inside and trying the phone again, but the surface was level here, and I knew how to change a tire. I'd done it a couple of times—in my teens. *Come on, Charlie. You can handle this.*

I went to the trunk and pushed aside Sophie's backpack and my duffle, retrieving my heavy coat. All I needed was to get chilled to the bone by the northerly wind that had picked up considerably since this morning. The spare was in its little compartment under the carpet, and I found the tire iron and jack. Thank goodness Ron hadn't robbed tools from the car for some other project.

It took me fifteen minutes to decipher the instructions in his owner's manual as to how and where to set the jack—sports cars are very different in that regard than Jeeps, I discovered. The wind was steadily picking up but I managed. Sophie stood by the roadside, hugging herself and looking very put out, but hey. I wasn't going to let her sit inside the car while I had it jacked up.

The spare was in place and I'd tightened three of the lug nuts when I sensed a car pulling off behind me. An Arizona state trooper climbed out, setting his Smokey hat on his head.

"You ladies need some help?"

I realized Sophie was standing there with her short skirt flipping around in the breeze, and this must have been what attracted his attention.

The officer quickly realized how young the girl was, so he turned his attention to the situation with the Mustang. I may be a modern woman but I'm no martyr. I stepped aside and let him finish attaching the lug nuts and positioning the flat tire in the trunk, then I thanked him for getting us out of the cold that much sooner. He responded with a tip of his hat and more advice about the approaching weather front.

We drove on, heading toward Holbrook where we would finally get off the interstate and onto some less traffic-heavy roads. Sophie went back to her very busy life of texting with friends, while I mentally reviewed the route, remembering the series of different highway numbers we would take next. I was debating the protocol for car travel with an unfamiliar passenger—would she object if I turned on the radio or, worse, tune it to a station I couldn't stand when I glanced at the dashboard and saw bright red letters. Check Engine!

Seriously? We should have been less than three hours into the trip and it was already mid-afternoon. I drove on for a few more miles. These things can short out, right? Maybe the light would just go away and solve all my problems. But no. It stayed on, staring steadily at me with that beady red eye.

I spotted an exit ahead and took it. About a half mile along the side road, stood a gas station that I only realized as I approached was decrepit and long out of business. Okay, no help there. But I could park out of the wind and make a call.

Ron answered on the second ring. I told him about the light and that we were about twenty-five miles from Holbrook. "Advice?"

"Don't keep driving. That thing came on last week and then went off. When I asked my regular mechanic, he said to bring it in the minute it came back on."

And you didn't think to tell me this? I growled and hung up on him. My mood plummeted as I debated calling roadside assistance again, but I did. This time the wait was only estimated to be thirty minutes. I handed my phone off to Sophie and demanded hers in return. She looked as though I'd just kidnapped her firstborn child.

"Stay on the line and give mine back if someone comes on," I instructed. "I'm going to search for alternatives."

I did a search for towing services in Holbrook, Arizona. Two garages came up and I tapped the number for the one with the most impressive ad. A male who sounded younger than Sophie answered.

"I need a tow truck sent to … hang on a second." I stepped out and tried to decipher the chipped and faded sign. "It's an old gas station off I-40 that's called something like Pecos Bill's."

"Um, I don't know where that is."

I wanted to ask if his father was there, but that seemed insulting.

"Besides, I'm here at the garage by myself and the only thing I know how to do is an oil change. I got two of those waiting before I can go home."

"How about someone else? Your online ad says you offer 24-hour towing."

"Yeah, that'd be my uncle Jeff. He had to take off for a funeral this afternoon. Won't be back because they're all going to Ryley's Pub after."

I thought of asking about the other tow service in town but figured that would be a waste of battery life on the phone, so I just thanked the kid and went back to my search page.

A woman answered this time. I went through the whole explanation of my problem and where I was, again.

"My husband drives the truck but he's not here right now."

"Please tell me he's not at Ryley's Pub."

"Huh? Oh, the Wilson funeral. No, he didn't much get along with old man Wilson. Oh—I see what you're saying. No, Tyler's out on another call. I can send him when he gets back."

"Have him call me first, just in case our roadside assistance sends someone." I gave her my number, then swapped phones with Sophie again.

It occurred to me that even if the helpful roadside assistance folks should answer, they would probably look up our location and do the very same thing I'd just done. They would learn that Jeff was out drinking, and Tyler would be available when he finished his previous job. But call me an optimist—I stayed on the line anyway.

"I need to charge my phone," Sophie said. "Is it okay if I plug it in?"

She was about to do so when I thought better of it. "It won't take a charge unless the engine is running, and that's not a good idea right now. Sorry."

She shot me a look, the kind teen girls pull off so well.

I glanced at the level of my own battery and decided I shouldn't stay on hold any longer. I found an option on the verbal menu that would let me leave a message for 'the next available associate' and went through my spiel. It was all I could do for the moment. Someone would surely get back to me soon.

An hour later—during which Sophie and I exchanged not more than forty words—my phone rang.

"It's Casey at ABC Towing. You still need your car brought in?" asked the woman I'd last spoken with.

"Yes! Absolutely, yes."

I heard her say something to someone in the background.

"Okay, we gotcha. Tyler's on the way. Should take him fifteen minutes or so."

It was more like twenty-five, but the sun was getting low in the sky now, and I was not going to quibble. The sight of a nice big tow truck was welcome, whenever it showed up. It backed up in front of our disabled car. The guy who climbed out was in his early forties, tall, with shoulders like a linebacker and a shock of dark hair, which he quickly covered with a knitted wool cap. He gave us a smile and gave the Mustang a quick once-over.

"Won't run at all?" he asked.

"It was doing just fine but then I got a light." I explained that I'd called Ron because this vehicle is his baby.

Tyler sat behind the wheel and turned the key. "Yep, it's still there. We'll get you to the shop and our mechanic can hook it up for a diagnostic check."

"We need to get to Mesa by tonight."

He shook his head. "Not gonna happen. Tom's at a funeral this afternoon and won't be back until morning. There's only one other shop in town."

I nodded. I knew how the rest of this story went.

He glanced toward Sophie, who was shivering in the

cold breeze. "You ladies can climb in the cab of my truck. It's all warmed up."

My young charge didn't need to be told twice. She was inside that truck in mere seconds.

Tyler walked to the back of the truck and, with the efficiency that comes from years of practice, had the crippled Mustang hooked up and sitting on the bed of the truck in under five minutes. We were on the road again—at last.

I chafed at the wasted afternoon. I could have pretended I didn't see the dashboard light come on, and we would have made it into Holbrook under our own steam. Or not. I reminded myself that we could have lost power in the middle of the traffic lanes and been in a far worse situation. And the bottom line was that the car still needed mechanical attention and wasn't going to get that until tomorrow morning.

My brain went into overdrive, considering alternatives. The best would be that I'd quickly find a rental car in Holbrook. I could leave the Mustang at the garage and complete the journey to Mesa in some other vehicle. Drop Sophie off with her mom, stay the night, then return the rental and pick up Ron's car tomorrow.

But I hadn't counted on just how small a town Holbrook really is. There was one main drag, lined with fast food places, two churches, an auto parts store, three gas stations. A couple of chain hotels sat near the I-25 ramp, and there were a couple of smaller ones. The street lights were already on, and I glanced at my watch. Four-thirty.

Okay, still doable. It might take an hour to arrange for a car and fill out insurance paperwork. And we ought to get something to eat. I realized the bag of Cheetos had vanished hours ago and my belly was growling. But with new wheels and food, we could still complete the trip by nine or so.

Did I want to? Not really. At home, I'm more of the tucked-in-after-dinner type. But, truthfully, I hadn't wanted to do this road trip at all. Best to just get it over with.

As it turned out, the spatters of rain on the tow truck's windshield decided it for me.

Chapter 4

Casey and Tyler must have been a long-time couple. They had that look about them. She was waiting behind the counter in the small auto repair shop, tapping keys on a calculator that had to be as old as I am. She looked up with a smile.

I posed my question about the availability of a rental car.

"Nothing like Hertz or Avis around here," she said. "Sometimes Josh Briner loans out cars. But, honey, have you heard the weather report?"

I admitted I hadn't.

"Rain's coming in heavy. And you said you're heading toward Payson? Likely to be snowy up there."

I thought of the raindrops we'd already encountered, but I still tapped into the weather app on my phone. What is it about modern life where we need a gadget to verify what's going on right in front of our faces? And yes, Casey's assessment seemed to agree. Rain, possibly turning to sleet or snow during the night.

Did I want to head out on a highway in a vehicle I wasn't familiar with, in conditions that could get iffy right away? Short answer—no.

Did I want to spend the night with a sullen teen and drag out my unwanted trip another day? No to that, as well.

Did I have much choice? Realistically, I could push through. But all of Drake's warnings about weather and dead pilots came rushing back at me. Better safe than sorry. I adjusted my expectations for how this job would go, and I turned to Sophie.

"Better grab our stuff," I told her.

Casey gave a smile of relief. "We're heading home for the night. We can give you a ride."

"I suppose we can get a room here in town easily enough."

A wrinkle crossed her forehead. "Don't bother with the Holiday Inn or La Quinta. I already know they're full, 'cause a big road rally group is in town. Bunch of fancy Corvettes traveling cross country together. They meant to make it as far east as Gallup tonight, but those sports cars aren't good on snowy roads, so they all pulled in here and filled up the good places. My sister's the manager at the Holiday Inn, and she told me by lunch time they were fully booked and sending people to the other."

Hm. "What are our other choices?" Even as I asked, I was searching on my phone.

"Well, the J&J Motel is generally clean and the people are nice. Indian or Pakistani, I'm not sure. Real polite. The

Sundowner, unfortunately, is a has-been. Real popular back in my parents' day but I wouldn't go there now."

Tyler had the Mustang safely stowed in one of the garage bays and Sophie was hefting her backpack out of the trunk. I phoned the J&J, only to be told they had no vacancies. And calls to the two chain places (yes, I knew it was silly optimism) gave the same answer. With a sigh, I told Tyler we'd need a ride to the Sundowner.

"I'd offer you a room at our house," Casey said, apologetically, as I grabbed my personal gear from the Mustang, "but all three kids have friends staying the night, and we're really maxed out."

"Hey it's no problem. If we can make a couple of quick stops for me to pick up a toothbrush and some fast food, I'm sure we can make do. It's only one night."

Famous last words.

We did our quick errands and arrived at the Sundowner. The couple offered to come into the motel's lobby, to make sure we got a room before leaving us on our own.

Casey glanced around as we walked through the door. "Could be the very same carpet," she muttered under her breath.

I held onto the hope that the rooms had been upgraded since the '70s as I handed over my credit card. We were given keys (yes, actual metal keys) to room 109, and bade Tyler and Casey goodbye while we pulled our bags out of their SUV.

"Call the shop in the morning, anytime after nine, and I'll let you know what the mechanic says." Casey's eyes were warm. "And here's our home number, just in case tonight … Well, if you need anything."

I squeezed her hand and shouldered the big duffle

bag with my so-called emergency gear. Unfortunately, this wasn't the type of emergency I'd packed for.

"Ew," Sophie said, nose wrinkled, when we stepped into the room.

I assumed her reaction was more about the brown carpeting and orange floral bedspreads than anything else. The air smelled of disinfectant with undertones of ancient cigarette smoke. At least I didn't spot any bugs diving for the shadows, even when I switched on the bathroom light. The surfaces all seemed clean enough and there was a band of paper stretched across the toilet seat. Very old school, for sure.

Just to be sure, I peeled back the bedspread and blanket. The sheets weren't exactly crisp, but everything looked and smelled clean enough. No insect life there, either.

"Okay. Well." I faced Sophie, who had gingerly set down her pack. "The electricity works so we can each charge our phones. I suppose that's the good news."

I sent off quick texts to both Ron and Drake. Stuck for the night but we're warm and dry. Here's where to come looking if we vanish.

Rethinking that last bit, I deleted it and just gave the name and location of the motel.

In addition to the two double beds and nightstand, the room contained a scarred dresser with an analog TV set atop it and a small round table with two chairs. We took seats and dug into the bag from Taco Bell, now lukewarm.

Once her initial hunger was satisfied, and with her phone plugged in way across the room, Sophie actually spoke to me.

"So how'd you get the job of taking me back to my mom?"

"Pure luck. I'm a partner in a private investigation firm, and I guess we were hired because … I'm not sure, exactly. My partner was otherwise obligated because of a court case. So, I got nominated."

"Huh. Private investigators. Is that like on those old TV shows? My mom watches *Mannix* and *Charlie's Angels* on one of those satellite TV channels."

I smiled and passed her another taco. "Their lives are a lot more action-filled than ours, I'm sure." But when I paused to think about it, I wasn't so sure. I've been shot at, had my home set on fire, my vehicle sabotaged, and was once a suspect for murder. Hm. Maybe *I* should be up for a TV role. Instead of telling her all this, I switched subjects.

"How did you choose New Mexico?"

She gave a blank stare.

"To run away to. Why Santa Fe?"

Her mouth pursed and one shoulder rose. "Dunno. Well, I didn't exactly choose Santa Fe. I caught a ride out of Mesa with some friends who were heading for Las Cruces, then I hitched my way north 'cause my mom knew these kids and where they were heading. I wasn't in the mood to be found."

My brain zipped through several responses. Hitchhiking—so dangerous, especially for a cute girl alone. Las Cruces is a college town and it would have been easy enough for her to blend in and find someone to crash with. And 'not in the mood'? She had to mean something more by that statement.

What I landed on was, "What happened next?"

"I was somewhere north of Albuquerque when my mom called. She was all, like, mad at me and demanding— where are you? All that shit. And I was all, like, what do you care? I hung up on her."

"Surely she cares what—"

"Look, she and the new guy had just got back from Las Vegas, and she didn't any more care about me than …" Her nose reddened and I wondered if she was about to cry. But she sniffed loudly and straightened her shoulders. "After that I just ignored her calls."

"They went to Vegas and left you on your own?"

"Yeah. No big deal. I've stayed on my own since I was ten."

In the eyes of the law, I was pretty sure leaving a ten year old, or even a thirteen year old, alone while the parents went out of town would be a pretty big deal.

"He's not even my dad. He's got no say over me." She wadded up her food wrappers and stood, heading into the bathroom.

She emerged wearing a pair of fuzzy pajama bottoms and a t-shirt and immediately went over to check her phone.

"Sophie—"

"I don't want to talk about it anymore." She flopped down on one of the beds. Thumbs in action once again, she was apparently deep in conversation with her friends.

I gathered the remains of our skimpy dinner and stuffed the wrappers and bag into the waste basket. Sitting cross-legged on my own bed, I checked email and answered Drake's text, feeling a little funny about carrying on anything like an intimate phone conversation with Sophie so nearby.

When I next noticed the time, it was only seven o'clock, but it felt hours later. I caught myself yawning, wanting to burrow in and make it a very early night. But I thought of how easily Sophie had managed to escape authority in the past. What would stop her from waiting until she heard a gentle snore from me, then taking off into the night?

Chapter 5

After checking the locks on the door, I'd pulled off my jeans intending to slip between the sheets in my underwear and shirt. Sophie had crawled into her bed thirty minutes ago, still staring at her phone screen while the throb of heavy music came through her earbuds. At least she seemed well settled for the night. I switched off the bedside lamp and rolled over.

Almost immediately I sensed activity. Sophie was still in her bed, the glow of her phone now coming from the nightstand. But flashing lights intruded around the edges of the curtain. I got up to check it out. Standing to one side, I peered toward the parking lot.

Directly outside our window sat a fire truck, lights flashing. My heart went into overdrive. *What the—*

A fireman sat in the driver's seat, making no move to

get out, and while I watched another in full uniform with reflective tape all over his coat, walked up to the driver. They appeared to be having a leisurely conversation, which calmed my pulse a little.

Then I glanced around the rest of the lot. At least a dozen emergency vehicles, including an EMT rig and a bunch of police cars, sat out there. Absolutely quiet. All lights flashing. I couldn't take my eyes away, and my imagination geared up.

Was there a guest with a medical emergency? Did they have a dangerous suspect cornered in one of the rooms? Were those SWAT teams? Why was there no action or shouting?

Behind me, Sophie's breathing had become soft and regular. A quick glance assured me she was settled in her bed, her phone dark and quiet on the nightstand.

I peered outside again. The parking lot glistened with water from the light rain that had begun to fall. Aside from the two standing beside the fire truck, I saw no people. Only flashing lights. It was so eerie I couldn't take my eyes away. When it became apparent that whatever the emergency, it didn't involve gunshots aimed at a guest room, I felt the urge to step out, to ask the two firemen what was going on. But something held me back. Here I was, in a strange town, possibly witnessing something I shouldn't see.

I paced to the bathroom door and back again. Eleven times. Each time, the scene outside was the same. I should just go out there, check it out.

No, you shouldn't. No matter what they say, it's none of your business.

Opening that door gives Sophie the perfect chance to escape.

Leave it—as I would say to my dog.

About the time all these thoughts had processed their

way through my mind, an exit procession began. One police car after the other pulled slowly out onto the street, going different directions. The fire truck followed at the tail end, leaving the motel and parking lot eerily quiet. The dry pavement beneath the vehicles soon became wet and it was as if none of this ever happened.

I crawled back in bed, knowing that by morning I would question whether or not I had dreamed it.

A short breathing exercise calmed me down and I yawned hugely before feeling the cloak of sleep drop over me. I was deep, deep in the middle of a dream about Drake taking me to Hawaii on a sort of second honeymoon—just about to get to the really good part—when a loud *bam-bam-bam* jolted me awake.

Sophie screamed. I flailed, whacking my hand on the corner of the nightstand. The clock said it was 4:19 a.m.

"Yowch—dammit!" I grabbed my hand, trying to take the sting out.

"Hotel security! We need to check your room!" came a male voice outside the flimsy door.

I wanted to pretend the room was unoccupied, but Sophie's scream and my curse had already revealed us.

"Ma'am, please open the door. We received an alert that your smoke alarm has gone off."

I scrambled around the end of my bed and peeked out by the edge of the curtain. There was a dark figure standing at our door, but I couldn't make out details, just a male in a bulky coat. For not the first time, I wished I'd taken more time to prepare for this cursed trip. Normally I carry my pistol in my car or travel bag and it's at my side in a hotel room. I've only drawn it once in that situation, but it's a comfort.

Eyeing the door and inadequate locks, I'd give anything to have it here now.

Knock-knock-knock. "Ma'am. We need to check the room. Now."

I finally found my voice. "There's no way I'm opening this door to a stranger in the middle of the night. I can assure you there's no smoke in here. We were sound asleep. Please leave now."

"I'm under orders to check. Here's my security badge."

Apparently, he was holding something up to the peephole but there was no way to read the information.

"Tell you what—I'll just call 9-1-1 and we'll have the police come and check it out."

"We can avoid that if you'll just—"

"No way! I'm dialing right now."

And like a dark ghost in the light from the parking lot, the man vanished.

His disappearance didn't exactly dispel my fears. We were still two women alone in a dump of a motel in a strange town, with no car. I debated actually calling the police, but what would they do? Same for calling Casey and Tyler, although Tyler could come out here and pick us up, maybe let us spend the rest of the night in Ron's car at the garage. That held little appeal either.

I picked up the somewhat grimy landline phone on the nightstand and pressed 0, on the vague idea that maybe a desk clerk really stayed in the office all night. A tinny ring sounded in the earpiece but no one answered. Imagine my surprise.

Sophie had turned on the bedside lamp and was curled into a tight lump against the headboard of her bed. I shrugged and hung up the useless phone.

"I don't know what that was about, but we're not going outside that door until full daylight," I told her.

She merely nodded.

I parted the curtain and gave a long look around the parking lot. Six cars sat outside various rooms. I didn't see any activity, and it was impossible to tell whether other room lights had come on, given the straight-line layout of the building. The one thing I did see was that an inch of snow had fallen since we went to bed.

Aside from the obviously beautiful things about snow, one nice benefit is that it leaves clues. I pulled on my jeans and fleece jacket and rummaged in my duffle for the flashlight I always carried.

"What are you doing?" Sophie demanded. "You said no leaving the room."

"I'm not going anywhere. You stay put."

I visually scouted the lot one more time from the safety of the window, then went to the door. As it opened inward, I aimed the light-beam at the ground. A muddle of footprints had packed the snow in front of our room. I took one step outside and shined the light up and down the sidewalk. The prints had come from the left, the direction of the motel office. Interestingly (scarily) they had not paused in front of any other door, only ours. When the man left, he'd apparently walked back in that direction but instead of going to the office, he'd cut across the parking lot and gotten into a vehicle that waited near the street. My skin rippled with goosebumps.

What on earth was that about?

I grabbed my phone and took a few pictures of the clearest footprints, then walked out to the car tracks. Clearly, it had driven in from the main street, after the snowfall, and had left in the same direction. I snapped shots of the tracks.

Back inside—with all the locks engaged—I looked over to Sophie, still huddled in the corner with her covers up to her chin.

"Are we safe here?" she asked.

I forced a cheery smile. "I think so. Whoever came was probably looking for someone else. They got in a car and drove away." I showed her the pictures. "See if you can get some more sleep."

She edged downward and I smoothed the sheet and blanket and tucked them around her. To show her how confident I felt, I slipped back into bed as well. But my brain wouldn't shut down, even with the light off and the world quiet again.

My reassurance that the early morning visitor was looking for someone else didn't quite add up. If that was the case, why did he call me Ma'am and why the ruse about a smoke detector? He would have called out the name of the person he thought was in the room. And what was all the earlier hoopla with the law enforcement vehicles and fire truck? Were the two incidents related in some way?

All I could say for sure was that I was plenty ready for daylight and to get back on the road again.

My eyes had closed for a while but I never did drift back into anything resembling blissful sleep. By six-thirty I was eager to be out of there, but wasn't due to check in with the garage until nine. I rolled out of bed and dressed. When I emerged from the bathroom, I saw Sophie was burrowed into her covers, lying on her side with her phone in hand.

"Get dressed. I'm going down to the office to check out and then we'll get some breakfast."

She grumbled something that sounded like the usual teen declaration that she didn't eat breakfast. I ignored it. She'd come with me if I had to put a leash on her and drag her along like a stubborn puppy. There was no way I was leaving her in the room alone for an hour or more. To guarantee she didn't make a run for it now, I picked up her coat and boots and carried them with me.

A middle-aged woman was this morning's clerk at the front desk. I began by asking for a receipt for the night's charges and followed up with something that had occurred to me around five o'clock.

"Someone came to our door in the early hours this morning. Sounded like he had the wrong room, but he didn't go along and wake up anyone else. Like he knew who was in there and was demanding we come out. Was our room rented the night before last? Or maybe the night before that?"

"That's 109? Um, yes, I believe so."

"Can you tell me who it was? This man was pretty scary. I'm planning to report the incident to the police."

Her eyes got wary at once. "Look, we don't need any trouble. The people in that room before you were a nice, older couple from Des Moines. Just traveling through, like yourself." The hint was plain: Keep on traveling through.

My smile was probably skeptical. "We're going to grab some breakfast. I'll turn in the key when we come back to pick up our things. Where's a good breakfast place, walking distance?"

"Lil's is always good, always busy. Great pancakes, huge

omelets. Two blocks farther west."

I folded my receipt and walked out the door. Did I believe her, about the couple from Iowa? Maybe. I couldn't see that she had a reason to lie. She definitely wanted to set aside my suspicions. I should have asked about the earlier light show, all those cop cars with strobes on. But she hadn't been on duty last night, and even if she'd heard about it I doubted she'd share information with me.

No one but my family and the tow truck owners knew where we were.

Unless …

Sophie was sitting on the edge of her bed when I walked in, her oversized t-shirt slipping off one shoulder, her hair tousled. I dropped her coat on the bed and the boots on the floor.

"Did you tell anyone where we stayed last night?" My tone probably came out grumpier than I intended.

"Just my mom, like you said."

"Fine, yeah. She was expecting us and we had to let her know. Anyone else?"

She shook her head but didn't quite meet my eyes as she stood up and shuffled off to the bathroom. I heard the shower start.

Chapter 6

There was one empty table at Lil's Café. Gracie Nelson and Penelope Fitzpatrick reluctantly took the six-top, Gracie telling the hostess they'd be happy to share if someone else came in.

"Sure, hon," the woman said. "Tell your mom thanks." She plopped two menus down while Pen surveyed the bakery case.

"She's not my—" Never mind, Gracie thought.

Actually, she would be proud to claim Pen as family. The older woman with classic Hollywood beauty and a trace of a childhood British accent had become the mother-hen to Gracie and the group of friends who'd banded together and solved several mysteries.

Pen took the seat across the table and picked up her menu. "Well, my dear, the scones are tempting but I believe

I'll check out the omelets."

Grace had already set her menu aside. "They've got Eggs Benedict, and you know what a sucker I am for that."

"They didn't have such dishes in Thailand, I take it?"

Gracie laughed. "Not hardly."

"Too bad the job didn't hold out longer."

"We were disappointed, but not heartbroken. Scott loved his work, but didn't care much for the lifestyle. I never did adapt to the heat and humidity."

"You're an Arizona girl. Heat doesn't faze you."

"Okay, then it was the humidity. Absolutely stifling. And the kids missed their friends. You know how teens are."

"Thankfully, I don't." Pen set her menu aside. "Know how teens are."

"Lucky you. Ah well, my two will be grown up before I know it, and I'll look back on these years fondly. Or not."

They both laughed. The waitress appeared and took their orders, then the two turned back to business.

"Do you think we'll find him here?" Gracie asked.

Pen stared out the window for a moment. "I don't envision him staying in a town this size. Strangers tend to get noticed in places like this. But we know he traveled through. Amber verified that from Linda Ratcliff's credit card statement. The card was used here as recently as yesterday."

"I agree. He'll get back to the Phoenix area. There, or Vegas. He has property, after all."

"I find that surprising—his penchant for holding on to real estate. Most grifters stay footloose, don't want the obligations that come with owning homes."

Gracie looked up to see the hostess approaching, a woman and a teen following her. At her question, they assured her it was fine for the new duo to share the table. Long habit had Gracie noticing details. The woman was in her thirties, with long auburn hair and hazel eyes. She wore jeans, a pullover sweater, and a fleece jacket. The teen was about her own daughter's age, with blonde hair to the middle of her back, deep brown eyes, and chin dimple. She'd overdone the makeup, especially the pouty lips.

"Thanks for sharing your table. I had no idea the restaurant would be so crowded," the woman said with a winning smile. "I'm Charlie, by the way. And this is Sophie."

Gracie felt an instant rapport with this Charlie. Even Sophie, eyes on her phone, thumbs typing away, reminded her of Kylie.

"What brings you to Holbrook, and out walking in the snow?" Pen asked.

Charlie went into a quick story about giving Sophie a ride to Mesa and the car breaking down nearby. "I'm hoping the garage mechanic can get us back on the road soon. The weather report shows it warming up, so I imagine the snow will be gone by midmorning. What about you? Are you here with the road-rally group?"

Gracie laughed. "Hardly. We're actually kind of informally on a case, tracking down a con man."

"Really? Okay, I have to know more. When you say *on a case …*"

"We're not licensed investigators or anything like that," Gracie said.

"But we have had some interesting experiences …" Pen poured a dollop of milk into the tea the waitress had brought.

"Like recovering stolen diamonds."

"Stealing them back," Pen reminded.

"Oh yeah, and stealing money … okay, actually, returning stolen money to the rightful owners."

Charlie's eyes sparkled now. "Money and jewels taken by con artists, I take it?"

"Exactly."

"And you are currently on a case like this?" Charlie took a moment to look up at the waitress and point to an item on the menu.

Once the orders were completed, Gracie took up the story. "We are. A friend of a friend—her name is Linda Ratcliff—got involved with a very charming man …"

"As they all are," Pen inserted. "Trust me, I know."

"She does," Gracie confirmed. "We've all had personal experiences, and that's how our team got together. Five of us. The Heist Ladies is what we call ourselves. Pen, myself, Sandy, Mary, and Amber."

Charlie lit up. "I love it! So … can you say more about this current case?"

Pen and Gracie exchanged a look. "I don't see why not. As long as you promise you aren't friends with this man and wouldn't tip him off."

"If I were friends with him and learned he'd ripped off an unsuspecting woman … I'd turn him in anyway."

Pen picked up the story. "Linda is in her eighties, and she became very lonely after her dear Roger passed. Somehow through a mutual acquaintance—we are not certain about the exact connection—she met Edward. To most of us who've known her a long time, it was a bit shocking how quickly they became an item."

"But he made her happy, they traveled all over the world, and she loved buying him nice things."

"Spent a bloody fortune on him, we're now learning."

"Yes, her daughter has recently become involved, trying to help straighten out Linda's finances. It looks like this man has pretty much cleaned out her life savings, everything she and Roger worked so hard for. He managed to get her to put his name on everything with a title—cars, life insurance, even her home."

"Well, he didn't quite get the house yet," Pen reminded. "But he was working on it, through wheedling his name into her will and trust documents."

"Shit. Sorry, I—"

"Don't worry, Charlie. We feel the very same."

"So, what can you do?"

"Pen has a dear friend who used to be the district attorney. He's hooked Linda up with a couple of good lawyers who can get all the titles changed back. We're trying to trace the money exchanges, and our friend Amber is tracking his movements through Linda's credit cards, and that's how we ended up here."

"She can do that?" Charlie held up a hand. "Don't answer. I don't want to get Amber in any trouble."

Plates arrived just then, filled with omelets, Eggs Benedict, and pancakes (with plain toast for Sophie), and their attention went to the food for a few minutes. The conversation turned toward the weather, then mutual connections. When the Ladies learned Charlie was from New Mexico, Pen mentioned that Amber's parents lived in Santa Fe—the usual 'small world' revelations that often come out during chance meetings.

"Well, this has been great fun," Charlie said, as she pushed her plate aside, "but we'd better call the garage and see if we can get on the road again. I'm hoping our car's problem is a simple fix."

"Look, if it's not ready," Gracie said, getting a nod from Pen, "I'm sure we could all fit easily into my minivan. As soon as we hear from Amber, we're likely heading back toward Phoenix today anyway."

Charlie appeared to consider it. "We couldn't ask that of you, running us around that huge city. Plus, I'd have to get back here to pick up the car later. We'll find something to rent if we have to."

"Take our numbers anyway," Pen insisted. "One never knows when having a friend will come in handy."

"If our transportation doesn't work out, you may be sorry you made that offer," Charlie said with a smile, as she entered Gracie's number into her phone.

"And if you encounter an Edward Peppard in your travels, be sure to let one of us know. We want that man *out* of society."

Chapter 7

Already the morning air was warming, and Sophie and I walked back to the motel through light slush. Traffic was moving well and the pavement was wet but not slippery. I felt my mood rise. Until I tapped in Casey's number.

The mechanic had run a diagnostic on Ron's car, and the fix was simple, just a computer chip. But the chip was nowhere to be had in this town and would need to be shipped in. Two days in the shop. I gave a sigh, but accepted Casey's offer of a ride to the local used car lot. Casey assured me they knew the owner, and he often provided short-term rentals. She would pick us up at the motel in ten minutes.

I found myself looking around as we walked up to room 109, still a little wary of the man who'd pounded on our door. But I didn't see any more tracks around the door than those we'd left earlier. Even those would soon be gone, as soon as the sun reached the sidewalk. We went inside, gathered our belongings, then turned in the key. True to her word, Casey pulled up right on time.

"If you don't need anything else out of the Mustang, I can take you directly to the car lot. I called ahead and talked to Josh, our friend."

The door to room 108 opened just then and an older man stepped out. "What the ever-loving hell!" He'd come to an abrupt stop on the doormat and was staring at the ground in front of his room. "My car's gone! Where in hell did my car go?"

I tossed my duffle into Casey's van and turned toward the man. He was quite elderly, but not a bit stooped. His white hair gleamed in the sunlight, and his blue eyes flashed with indignation. His veined hand held a bowling ball bag.

"Maybe you parked it somewhere else?" I suggested.

"I know where I parked my car, miss. It was right here in front of my room." The bag dropped to the sidewalk.

Sure enough, there was a vehicle-sized clear square on the asphalt where the snow had not fallen. A set of tracks showed that it had backed out, but since the rest of the parking lot snow was quickly melting, it was impossible to tell where it had gone.

"If you're absolutely sure you didn't move it, you should report this to the police. I'm sure they'll find it quickly in a town this size." I knew, the moment I said it, that was silly. Holbrook, right on the major east-west thoroughfare that is I-40, would be one of the easiest places on earth for a stolen car to vanish from. "At least if the police have the details, they can put it on a watch list or something."

Suddenly, the clear blue eyes weren't so sure, the

upright spine slumped a bit. "What am I gonna do? I have to get back to Jeannie."

Casey had stepped out of the van. "Sir, let's think about this. This is Charlie, by the way, and Sophie, and I'm Casey. What's your name?"

"Harvey Molson."

"And who is Jeannie?"

"My *wife*. My wife of sixty-five *years*."

"Where is Jeannie? She's not traveling with you?"

The eyes grew sad. He shook his head slowly. "I just drove over to Gallup to visit an old hunting buddy for a couple of days. She can't travel anymore. My Jeannie is in a care home."

We waited a beat for more specifics, but eventually I had to ask. "Where is this care home, Harvey?"

"Phoenix."

"And the name of it?"

His eyes darted back and forth. "I gotta get back there. She misses me when I'm not there."

Surely he would remember the name of the place in a few minutes, once he wasn't concentrating so hard on remembering.

Casey spoke up. "Why don't you come with us, Harvey? These ladies are about to rent a car because theirs is broken down. You could do the same, and report yours missing at the same time. We can help. Where are the rest of your things?"

He stooped and picked up the bowling bag. "This is it."

Hm, classy luggage. I suppressed a smile.

We all piled into Casey's vehicle and she headed toward the business district of town. Passing curio shops that touted their selections of petrified wood, a "boutique" of second-hand clothing, two gas stations (which I noted displayed prices far less than on the touristy route), and a pawn shop, we came to an intersection with a used car lot on the corner. Casey pulled in and drove up to the small wooden building that served as an office.

We'd been spotted because a man stepped out before the van had come to a complete stop. Josh was probably in his early forties, although he had that youthful air and might be closer to fifty. His buffalo-check shirt was topped by a puffy vest, and his Timberland boots were more suited for hiking than for impressing potential auto customers. He ran a hand through his collar-length hair and smiled at Casey. I got the feeling Casey, Tyler, and Josh had known each other since elementary school.

She introduced us, including Harvey, basically ignoring Sophie because the girl was ignoring the rest of us.

"I've got an '09 Highlander on the lot that might suit your needs," he told me as we walked down the first row of vehicles. "Real low mileage, and she's been freshly detailed." He stopped beside the mid-sized SUV, a sage green basic five-seater with a generous cargo area in back.

"I just need to get Sophie delivered to her mom in Mesa, then I'm turning around to come back and pick up my regular ride."

"This one'll do that easy. And it's got automatic four-wheel-drive in case you run into any snow on the roads in the mountains."

I nodded agreement. It seemed perfect for my mission.

Harvey had followed along and was now shifting his weight from one foot to the other. "I'll be needing something too." He repeated his former rant about his car being stolen from the motel lot, but Josh quickly steered him toward the practicalities, asking if he'd reported the theft to the police, mentioning that he'd need to file an insurance claim.

"Yeah, yeah, I know. Right now, I just gotta get another car and get back to my Jeannie."

We'd been walking back toward the small office and Josh ushered us inside. He pulled out a yellow tablet and wrote down the information about the green Highlander—the most informal rental agreement I'd ever seen. He photocopied my driver's license and insurance card while Harvey kept talking, and I signed the yellow sheet as a receipt for the SUV. The whole transaction seemed very trusting, but then I figured the garage could hold Ron's Mustang hostage until the used vehicle was returned, so they didn't have a whole lot to worry about.

I was busy putting away my identification cards and sticking the key to the rental in my jacket pocket, but I found myself listening in on the exchange between Josh and Harvey. I got the distinct feeling Josh had no intention of renting a vehicle to the old man, but he was going through the motions of politeness.

Harvey had pointed out a gigantic white pickup truck, which seemed way too much for a man of his slight stature to handle, and Josh politely asked for his driver's license.

"Oh, look man. Your license has expired. My insurance won't let me rent to anyone over 75, either. I'm real sorry." He'd finally found his way out of making a deal without seeming cruel.

"Bu- but … what'll I do? I gotta get back to Jeannie." Harvey sent an imploring look out to all of us.

No one had an answer. I really felt for the old guy. There was only one clear solution, although I knew I would live to regret it.

"Harvey, you should come with me and Sophie. We're heading toward Phoenix anyway …"

The three of us transferred our bags to the Highlander. I turned to Casey before getting behind the wheel. "Two days, max, right?"

She nodded. "Our mechanic ordered the part this morning. As long as the overnight shipping doesn't let us down, we'll have it installed on the Mustang by tomorrow afternoon."

Adding that *as long as* disclaimer did nothing to bolster my confidence. So far, this entire road trip had been a matter of what can go wrong will go wrong. Murphy's Law in action. But there was nothing to be gained by worrying. I climbed behind the wheel, with Harvey beside me and Sophie in the back. The Toyota started beautifully and we were off.

Chapter 8

I kept a close eye on our surroundings as we drove out of Holbrook. Despite all the activity this morning—meeting the Heist Ladies over breakfast, making the alternate car arrangements, and taking on a second passenger—I couldn't get the image of that man at our motel door out of my head. He had specifically come to that motel, to our room, and he left when I threatened to call the cops. Maybe we were not his target. But I couldn't let go of the idea that maybe we were.

A blue Chevy, which had been parked in front of the pawn shop across the street from the car lot, pulled into traffic behind me, staying a couple of car lengths back. It wasn't until the driver pulled into the drive-up lane at a bank that I wrote off that one as a tail. Two other vehicles stayed with us for short distances, but they also turned away well before I needed to make the turn to highway 377, which would take us into Heber and eventually Payson.

Three hours to Mesa and I'd at least be able to leave Sophie with her mother. Then I would need to figure out what to do with Harvey. I felt for him. But, like finding a stray puppy with a sad story and a winsome look, it didn't mean I wanted to adopt him. I glanced over to the passenger seat. He'd dozed off, his chin resting on his chest.

My thoughts drifted back to the conversation over breakfast, to the women and their search for this Edward Peppard. Something that had slipped my attention came back to me now.

"Sophie?" I glanced at my rearview mirror and saw her head bobbing to some tune coming through her earbuds.

I shoved my right arm between the front seats and tapped her on the knee, receiving a scowl in return.

"I need to ask you something."

She seemed put out at having to pause her music and remove one of the buds, but she eventually looked up.

"When we met those ladies at the restaurant, something they said seemed to catch your attention."

A shrug. But her eyes shifted sideways.

"They gave the name of that man they're tracking and you reacted. Edward Peppard."

I watched and saw the same stiffening of posture, the flicker of recognition on her face.

"Sophie, you know something about him. If you'll tell me about it, we can share it with Pen and Gracie, and maybe they can catch him."

Her face, still with its youthful softness, twitched. Only a little, but I caught it. I also drifted slightly over the center line on the road and shifted my attention away from the mirror.

"Sophie …?"

Some slight shuffling against the cloth car seat. "He goes by Eddie. Mom calls him *Dee*. So sickening."

"So … what … he's your mother's boyfriend? I think you mentioned earlier that she had a new man in her life."

"What*ever*."

"Sophie, it's important. Can you stick with me and give some kind of valid information here? If this is the same Edward Peppard that the Heist Ladies are looking for, he could be out to rip off your mom, same as he did that other lady. You don't want to see that happen, do you?"

"My mom's pretty savvy."

I wanted to deliver a lecture on how quickly even the most savvy woman can lose it when there's a guy with a convincing line and the sex is great, but that was probably too much information for a thirteen year old.

"Do you know where this Eddie is now? I mean, do you think the ladies were right, or do you know for a certainty that he's somewhere with your mom?"

There went the shoulder shrug again. "How would I know?"

I let a minute go by. "So, I'm getting the feeling Eddie isn't your favorite person of all time?" I turned halfway in my seat to let her see that I was smiling.

Her mouth twitched upward, just a little. "Not hardly."

"And your mom—is she serious about him? In love with him?"

"I don't know. They were all weird for each other in the beginning but then they started fighting a lot. He started trying to act like a dad, boss me around. That's when I left."

"Do you think … I mean, is it possible that he was the

person who came to our motel door last night?" Even as I asked, I knew how logic-defying that would be. This man figuring out that Sophie was with me and we were in that particular room.

Her answer surprised me. "Could have been, I suppose."

"When we get to the next stop, I'm going to call Gracie and let her know about this. It sounds like they have contacts, and maybe there's a way the information could help them."

"Whatever." And with that the earbud went in and she was back in Sophie-world.

So thankful I never had kids.

"Jeannie and I never had any, either," came a sleepy voice from the passenger seat.

Had I voiced that thought aloud? I needed to remind myself that I wasn't in the car alone or only with Freckles this time.

"Did you get a little nap, Harvey?"

"Oh, no. I never sleep during the day."

Uh-huh. The snores and that little bit of drool down the chin were done just to fool me.

"We'll be in Payson in about thirty minutes. You hungry?" It occurred to me that although I'd had a big breakfast, Sophie had only opted for toast, and I'd never even checked with Harvey. Of course, I hadn't known the old gentleman would become part of our little travel party, either.

"I could eat."

We went back and forth with ideas for a minute, with Harvey's vote being for a Whopper at Burger King. Finding the popular burger place was easy enough and we all piled out of the Highlander, went inside, and ordered lunch. Harvey went for the full deal—the biggest burger, large fries, and a gigantic soda. Looking at his slight frame and then watching him at the table, I have to admit to being surprised he could pack away that much food.

"Gotta visit the little boys room," he announced, a little too loudly, after sucking down the last of his soft drink.

"We'll be out in the car," I said.

Sophie, once she realized Harvey was buying, had shifted her focus from the cheaper items and opted for a fairly hefty lunch. She carried her fries out to the rental and established that she would be the front seat passenger for this leg of the trip. "You'll need directions to my house," she pointed out. And it was true, since the older vehicle didn't have built-in navigation.

"What we were talking about earlier," I said, "the fact that your mom's boyfriend is the man Pen and Gracie are looking for … I'm going to call them. You okay with that?"

She gave a half-hearted nod and stuffed three fries into her mouth.

Chapter 9

Gracie's phone rang and she took a second glance at the unfamiliar 505 area code before the name clicked. Charlie Parker. They'd met over breakfast, less than six hours ago.

"I may have a lead for you on Edward Peppard," Charlie said without preamble. "Are you still in Holbrook?"

Right to the point. Gracie liked that.

"We are." She was sitting in her van outside the Holiday Inn, while Pen had gone inside to use one of their tried-and-true maneuvers to locate the man.

They'd started at one end of town and worked their way to the other, using a variety of plausible sounding excuses: *My son called from Holbrook but didn't say what hotel he's in; my older brother has a heart condition and I'm worried; or the no-explanation version—can you ring this guest's room.* Whether the desk clerks cooperated or not, the bottom line was that they'd not found him.

"Charlie, please tell me you know where he is, and please let it be five minutes from here."

Charlie's pleasant chuckle came over the line. "I wish."

Pen walked up to the van, opened the passenger door, and slid inside, shaking her head to say she'd had no luck at this hotel either. "Charlie, I'm going to put you on speaker so Pen can get your news at the same time."

"Hello, Charlie. There's news?" Pen asked.

"Yes, and Sophie was the one who gave me some great information. We're in Payson, making a lunch stop, and I'm going to add her to the call if that's all right with everyone."

Gracie could hear some whispered exchange in the background, as though Charlie was perhaps having to convince Sophie to talk with them, but in a few seconds the girl said a reluctant hello.

"Hey, Sophie. How's it going?"

"Okay, I guess."

Gracie pictured her own daughter. Kylie was maybe a year older than Sophie, and while she hadn't been quite this moody, every teen had some type of attitude. She put on her friendly-mom voice. "So, you excited to be getting home, to see your mom again?"

"Yeah, I guess."

"Well, it had to be hard being on the road for months. One of my daughter's friends went through that. She told me it felt really good to be back in her own bed after the adventure."

She wasn't getting through. She could tell.

Pen chimed in. "Sophie, Charlie says you have something important for us?"

Charlie spoke up again. "This Edward Peppard you mentioned. Sophie recognized his name when you said it earlier and she'd been thinking about that. We think her mother has become involved with him. She could be his next target."

"Oh my gosh, Sophie. That could be a big break in our case," Gracie said. "Do you think he's in Holbrook?"

A whispered prompt in the background. "Go ahead and tell them."

"He could have been," Sophie said, a little shyness in her voice. "Someone came to our motel door and knocked, like, really loud."

"Did you see him?"

"Not really. But his voice seemed kind of familiar."

Charlie spoke again. "Whoever it was came up to our door, pounded, then left when I threatened to call the police. He drove away. *But*—the real news is that Edward Peppard has been living with Sophie's mom, Dixie O'Connell, in Mesa. The relationship has taken a downward turn and Sophie says it's part of the reason she left home."

"Did Edward ever mistreat you, Sophie?" Gracie's voice was a little sharp.

"No, not really. He can be really nice. He was always buying me stuff, like my new earbuds. It's just I heard Dee and Mom arguing a lot. I didn't like it."

"Sophie says he goes by Eddie, and her mother's nickname for him is Dee."

"Have you talked to your mom recently, sweetie?" Gracie asked. "Is he still there?"

"Um, yeah. Mom says Dee went to Vegas on business last week but she was expecting him back."

Gracie turned to Pen. "So he could have been here last

night, traveling through."

Pen nodded.

"I doubt Eddie would remain in Holbrook," Gracie said, as much to herself as to the rest of them. "We should head for Mesa and see if he's returned. Can you give us your mother's address, Sophie?"

A long moment of silence went by before Charlie spoke again. "I have the address but Sophie is worried about giving it out. I see what she's saying—if two women show up looking for Eddie, he may make a run for it. Either that, or Dixie may help to hide him. The relationship sounds complicated, to say the least. That's about all I can say right now."

With the teen girl right there in the car.

"How about if Sophie and I go there first? We're just a couple hours away. I'll see to it that Sophie and her mom are safely reunited, and I can find out if Eddie is actually there. At that point, I can play it by ear. Shall I call you? Should I bring in the police?"

"Calling the police won't help. He hasn't actually been charged with anything, so there's no warrant out for his arrest. He's slick. If he even admits to knowing our friend Linda, he'll have a story and the police will be helpless." Gracie realized how thin their case sounded.

Pen added, "Our friend Sandy lives in Mesa. She'd be the closest of us to the situation. I do think you're right, Charlie. Let's play it by ear once you arrive there."

"And, Sophie? You be careful, young lady. We don't want our youngest super sleuth to be in any danger," Gracie said. "As a mom myself, I'm ordering you. Careful."

They ended the call and Gracie turned to Pen. "What do you think? We head back to the valley?"

"We've had no luck at the hotels here. It's not as if we can go door to door, even though it's a small town. Yes, I have a feeling Holbrook is a dead-end trail."

Chapter 10

Harvey returned from the restroom. Amazing how long it can take an old man to pee, I thought. He stood on the sidewalk outside Burger King, staring around, and I realized he probably didn't remember what our Highlander looked like. I stepped outside my door and gave a shout. He perked up and walked right over.

I didn't imagine the look that crossed his face when he realized Sophie had taken over the shotgun seat, but he was gentlemanly enough to smoothly switch to the back. Five minutes later we were cruising through Payson and on our way again.

The higher elevation had received more snow than Holbrook, but even here it had now melted off the roadway, remaining only in the shaded areas beside buildings. As we left the town behind, I breathed a sigh; today's leg of the road trip was off to a better start than yesterday's. I wanted to find a chance to phone Drake, see how things were going at home, and fill him in on the fact that I was still a day away from a happy return.

"Gracie would be a cool mom," Sophie said, out of the blue. "I mean, I bet she is. She has two kids about my age."

I turned and smiled at her. "Yeah, I bet she is."

"Sometimes … well, once in a while I wish my mom would set boundaries like that. Tell me to be safe."

"She doesn't do that?"

"Not really. She's fun, though. All my friends think so." She was picking at a cuticle. "You'll see when you meet her."

I had no idea what to expect and found myself a little nervous. Sophie fiddled with her phone a little, but we must have reached an area with sparse signals as we descended a series of wide curves in the road, leaving the higher elevations of the north. She set the phone in her lap and stared out the side window.

"Look, I'm not a mom and I'd probably be a terrible one. But I need to ask you … what you said earlier about Gracie's caution. Do you have any reason at all to feel that you wouldn't be safe, returning home? Cause if you do, please tell me. We could figure out something."

There are so many stories of kids being abused or molested by a mother's new boyfriend, and with Sophie's budding young body and at a time when she might be exploring her own sexuality … I had to acknowledge there could be cause for concern. She was back at work on the cuticle again and I noticed it was getting raggedy. I'd begun to think she was slipping back into her previous sullen silence when she finally spoke.

"It's not really unsafe, but …"

Wait for it. Just let her speak in her own time. Even though I wanted to start grilling her.

"The fights were getting worse. Mostly about money. I guess Mom got some good money when my dad died."

A story way too similar to the one Pen and Gracie had told about their friend.

"She let him move in and now she can't get him to leave."

"She wants him to?"

"I heard her say so. There was a big fight. But then he goes back to being all charming and nice right away, and she can't stand up to him."

"Saguaro!" Harvey's exclamation from the back seat startled me. I'd nearly forgotten we had him with us.

Sophie turned in her seat and stared at him.

"It's a game Jeannie and I always play on road trips. First one to spot a saguaro shouts it out."

"Because …"

Sophie's tone told me her family had never played road games—I Spy, Alphabet, White Horse. And here was a new one—Saguaro. When I was a kid it was a great way our parents had to keep us busy and take our minds off the ever-present 'are we there yet?'

"Tell us about the game, Harvey," I suggested, because there was really nothing better to do at the moment.

"Saguaros only grow at certain elevations. That's why you never see them in New Mexico. Elevation's too high there. And Northern Arizona. Too high there too. But once we head south, off the Rim, we start watching. There's a point, after you've left the pine trees behind, where you'll start to see prickly pear—then you know you're getting closer. But you gotta get below, maybe 1200 feet or so. That's when you'll see the first saguaro."

I supposed I'd never thought about it. I knew I'd never seen the tall cactus with their interesting arms in my home state. They're fairly unique to the Sonoran Desert areas in Arizona, but I never gave any thought as to why that was so. I thanked Harvey for the little botany lesson.

"Another fun fact," he said. "They're a protected plant here in Arizona. Killing one is illegal."

I looked around and began to see hillsides full of them, like fields of telephone poles almost. "There are millions. Why would they be endangered?"

"Ah. I didn't say endangered. I said *protected*. You can dig them up and move them, which is how so many people have them as landscape plants. But don't chop one down. That's a bad deal."

"Well, that's good to know." Although I'd never in my life had a desire to chop down a monster cactus, I would keep it in mind.

Even Sophie seemed intrigued by the new information; she and Harvey bantered back and forth as they spotted more of the cacti, commenting on the unusual ways their limbs grew and twisted. He seemed intimately familiar with the area, as he pointed out narrow gullies and turnoffs to places where he'd gone hunting and fishing in his younger days. For a man who couldn't come up with the name of the place his wife currently lived, he was amazing with older details. Either he'd created a fictional story to get a ride with us, or he genuinely had better recall of yesteryear than of yesterday.

Traffic had picked up considerably and I realized it was now Friday afternoon, that time of the week when it seems all city dwellers are trying to get out, and all country dwellers are rushing to the city for shopping and entertainment. Fifth-wheel RVs and boats pulled by angry-looking pickup trucks dominated, and I supposed we were on the route to a popular lake or campground.

At home, late November isn't the time for camping but I had to remind myself that southern Arizona was just getting into prime snowbird season. I tuned out the chatter within the Highlander and concentrated on not getting pushed off the road by the other, super-aggressive drivers.

"Charlie …" I felt a tap on my arm. Sophie gave a head-tilt toward the back seat.

"There's an exit up here in about a mile," Harvey said. "I need another pit stop."

I guess I had ignored all other conversation long enough that I hadn't heard him the first time or two. My head was pounding, eyes blurry from concentrating so intently, and my irritation with the traffic . A break wouldn't hurt me either. I signaled and left the highway, following Harvey's directions to a gas station with a convenience store—which he hadn't mentioned was at least another fifteen miles out of the way. I stifled an unkind remark and just kept going. When we arrived at the charmingly named Punkin Center, I decided it wouldn't hurt to top up the tank anyway. I had no idea how many miles the trusty Highlander would be carrying us through the big city.

I pumped gas—only eight gallons—then headed inside to the little store. Something cold, fizzy, and caffeinated would probably help my headache and perk up my increasingly grumpy attitude. More than once today I'd wished for a magic lantern that would transport me back home in front of my own fireplace with my sweet puppy on my lap, rather than battling traffic while delivering two people I didn't know into a situation I couldn't even guess at.

The fountain drinks were in a little station at one side of the store, and I served up a big cup of ice and Coke. I didn't see any sign of Harvey. Still relieving himself, I supposed. Sophie had declined the offer of food or drink, so I headed on my own to the checkout counter.

Two clerks were on duty, one waiting on an elderly lady as she counted through a handful of coins. The other was a young kid who looked to be in his late teens—dark hair to his shoulders, tattoos running the length of both arms and crawling up his neck, tiny silver rings through an eyebrow and one nostril. He waved me over.

"That's all you've got, the drink?"

"Yeah." I dipped a hand into the depths of my purse and came out with a couple dollars.

"That's okay, I got it for you." He flashed me the sweetest smile.

"What—really? You don't have to do that."

"I know. You just look ready for a little act of kindness."

Aww … "You're so right. And you have brightened my day, for sure."

I didn't know what to do with the dollar bills in my hand, so I slipped them into the change-cup near the register. "Here. We'll pay it forward, in case someone else needs their day perked up, too."

The sweet smile again. "You have a great day."

I couldn't help but smile back. I wasn't sure that the rest of the day would be *great*, exactly, but he had definitely eased it along into becoming better. At the exit, I glanced out to see Harvey ambling across the parking lot to the car. Sophie was still in the front seat, her phone up to her ear.

Chapter 11

So what did he say?" Sophie was saying when I got back behind the wheel.

I started the SUV and pretended I wasn't blatantly eavesdropping as I glanced around to make sure everyone had seatbelts on.

"Where are you now?" From the tone of Sophie's voice, it sounded as if she was talking to her mother. "But he won't—" Head nodding. "Okay, yeah. I know."

I backtracked and aimed toward the highway once more.

"Probably an hour … half hour?" Sophie looked toward me, but I could only shrug. I'd never driven this route before.

The call ended and Sophie slumped in her seat.

"She's eager to see you, huh?"

"Yeah, way eager. She just called. She sounded kind of different." She stared out the side window.

"So you think we're an hour away, or less?"

"I guess." And the non-communicator was back.

I sipped my Coke and stayed in the right lane to let the crazy ones pass me, and a little of the earlier tension slipped away. I drummed up a fantasy in which we pulled up in front of Sophie's home, Dixie met her with open arms, Harvey remembered the facility where his wife was, and it happened to be three blocks from Sophie's home. By dinnertime, I would be settled into a nice hotel, enjoying the spa and ordering the best dinner on the menu, while billing it to the department that had sent me on this fun-filled excursion.

Of course, you *know* it … a fantasy is only that.

A slight bit of relief from the traffic came when we exited at Gilbert Road and made our way to Brown. Sophie directed me to make a turn into a subdivision of cute little houses with tile roofs and varying shades of tan stucco. Cookie cutter in an adorable sort of way. I pulled up in front of the one she pointed out.

"I don't see a car," I commented as I parked at the curb. "Does your mom keep it in the garage?"

She debated, as if this was a hard question. "Um, she said she was running to the store. She must not be back yet."

"We can wait a little while. Text her and let her know we're here."

She complied. Fifteen minutes went by with no response.

"I'm sure you have a key," I said, "but I can't leave you here alone. I'm supposed to be certain that you and your mom connect."

She shot me a look.

"You ran away once and it's cost the government a lot of money to get you back to this point. Sorry, but those are my orders. Plus, there's paperwork she needs to sign."

She at least had the good grace to seem a little embarrassed about the money aspect of it.

"Back in my day—" Harvey's tale got cut off by glares from both of us females.

"Thanks, but that doesn't matter," I said, as gently as I could. "Sophie, give your mom a call."

Dixie knew we were coming. Why the hell wasn't she here to meet us?

I watched Sophie tap a contact on her phone screen and wait for an answer.

What if Dixie was drunk, passed out on her couch while we sat out here? What if the happy home she'd portrayed to the authorities didn't exist and Sophie had run off for a legitimate reason? I knew nothing about the situation other than an assumption that the Child Services folks had checked this out, at least thoroughly enough to believe they were sending the girl back to a decent home.

"We should go in, Sophie. Get your key out."

"Um, well, I guess I lost it."

"Want to dig through your pack to be sure?"

"I could, but I kind of know where I lost it. A couple months ago? When I got to Las Cruces with my friends … I was so happy to get away that I threw my key in the river."

Talk about cutting ties. "Okay then. Is there a hidden key somewhere? Under the mat, one of those fake rock things …"

The girl shook her head.

"I'm going to check. You keep trying your mom's phone."

Harvey got out and trailed me to the front door, a reminder that delivering Sophie home was only half the task facing me today. I rang the doorbell and waited with scant hope. No sound from inside. I lifted the doormat—nothing. Shifted two flowerpots near the door. Nothing there either, which was something of a relief. Those would have been the most obvious places for thieves to find the key. I stepped back and surveyed the layout.

There was no code box near the garage door, and the handle didn't operate the door either. It was remote push button or nothing. A side gate led to a back yard. I bypassed two trash receptacles, the kind homeowners have to wheel out to the curb certain days of the week. The green one was marked with the universal symbol for recycling. The side gate opened easily enough and I found myself—along with Harvey—in a small yard that seemed lovingly tended. A porch swing, barbeque grill, two chairs with soft cushions, and a variety of flowering plants decorated the covered patio. Around the perimeter walls were raised beds with rosebushes, clematis, and honeysuckle, a green oasis in a city that favored sage and cactus for yard decoration.

Offhand, I couldn't see a reason why Sophie felt she needed to escape this place, but I also realized it's rarely the physical surroundings that cause unhappiness. Once again I came around to wondering what her home life had been like, especially with Eddie Peppard in the picture.

The sound of a vehicle starting grabbed my attention. I'd left Sophie alone in the Highlander, and the key was probably in the ignition. Yikes. I shoved my way past Harvey and ran to the front of the house. She was there. The vehicle in motion was in front of the next door neighbor's place. I let out a sigh and walked up to the open passenger window.

"Any word from your mom?"

She shook her head, holding up the phone screen so I could see a series of outgoing texts and none coming back.

"You talked to her a little over an hour ago, and she assured you she would be here."

Eyes shifting away from me.

"Sophie? She did say that, right?"

"Kind of."

If she were my own kid, I'd throttle her. However ... I made my voice as gentle as I possibly could. "What, *exactly*, did she say?"

"Um, she's with some friends ..."

"Eddie?"

"I'm not sure."

"Okay, so where is she, with these friends?"

"I'm not sure."

"Sophie ... take a guess."

"Well, sometimes they go down to Rocky Point ..."

"Where's that?"

"It's a cool little town with a beach and everything."

"A beach. As in, near the ocean." I felt my teeth grinding.

"Yeah. It's a half-day drive or so. In Mexico. We could totally go down there, like, easy."

"No. There's no way. Even if we had passports with us—which we don't—there's no way I'm heading into Mexico with someone else's kid and an old man who ... Never mind."

"You are, like, the least fun person I ever knew."

Coming from her, that didn't even hurt. Much. I am a completely fun-loving person, aren't I? Okay, maybe not under Sophie and Dixie's definition of fun. I'm sure Gracie and Pen could have handled this much better than I.

"I'm stepping away from this conversation for a moment. Keep trying your mother. Try phoning. We have to come up with an answer."

I walked back to the front door and pounded on the frame of the screen, then rang the doorbell six times in a row. It didn't bring a response but made me feel a tad less like I would explode.

Pulling out my phone, I tapped in the number Elena Garcia had given me. A recorded voice told me it was after hours at Social Services and I should call back. That meant Monday morning. Three days. Ugh. Had she provided me a personal number? I honestly couldn't remember. Maybe the form I'd signed would have one.

I stomped back to the Highlander, yanked open the door, and ripped my purse from the spot where I'd stashed it. Sophie's brown eyes were wide. I guess she figured out that she was on thin ice with me.

Pawing through the contents of the purse yielded nothing. Okay, what next? What about leaving Sophie with a neighbor?

"We really don't know most of them," she said, when I asked.

"Do you know *any* of them? Anyone your moth— Make that, anyone the social services lady would allow me to leave you with?"

"Not really." Sophie perked up and turned her attention to the phone in her hand. "Mom? Hey. We've had a hard time getting through."

I waggled my fingers, demanding the phone from her.

"Ms. O'Connell? Hi, it's Charlie Parker here. I'm sure Elena Garcia told you I'd be delivering Sophie home today, and we're here now. Not getting an answer at the door."

"Oh, really? Eddie told me he'd be there. Guess he forgot." If it's possible for a grown woman to sound exactly like a teenager over the phone, this was it. I almost began to think Sophie and a friend were pranking me. "Dee's normally so reliable, and he's just *so* great …"

I got the implication. Yeah, this was no teen.

"Dixie, where are you right now? Sophie said you'd just stepped out for some shopping?"

Her response was garbled, that watery sound that comes over cell phones sometimes. I asked her to repeat.

"… leave her there. She'll be fine until—" And then the call died. I hit redial immediately but nothing happened.

"I know a way to break in," Sophie offered helpfully. "My bedroom window faces the back yard and I've taken the screen off lots of times."

I was about to ask her what part of 'no, I'm not leaving you alone' she didn't understand, but Harvey emerged from the back just then, a pair of garden shears in hand.

"I found these, so I deadheaded the roses. Thought maybe something out front needs trimming too." He looked toward the potted plants on the front porch.

My headache was blossoming into a full-blown, throbbing nightmare.

Chapter 12

Charlie, Charlie, Charlie. Stop and think! But the only thing I could bring to mind was that the sun had just dipped below the houses to the west, I was sitting here in an unfamiliar neighborhood with a kid who should not be my responsibility and an old man who was blissfully cutting flowers. At least Harvey hadn't become stressed over finding his wife during the last couple of hours. Still, I was the one who would have to figure this out.

Food couldn't hurt. Unlike Harvey, I'd settled for only a few fries at lunch time, and that surely wasn't helping my headache or disposition. I rounded up my ducklings and headed back toward an Applebee's I'd spotted on our way in. The server fussed over delivering beverages to the table and suggesting numerous extras. I was not unhappy when he finalized our order and left us alone.

Both Harvey and Sophie sensed I wasn't in the best mood. They chatted quietly while I hunched in my chair, texting grouchy messages to my brother for getting me into this. Typical of Ron, he offered no sympathy, just a couple of 'did you try this?' suggestions.

One of the better ones was to get Harvey to go through his wallet. It could be that he'd have a business card or something else to identify the home where his wife was living. At least his driver's license—expired or not—should have his home address. With that, I'd have a place to deliver him and could be in charge of one less person for the evening.

Our food arrived, I made myself relax and enjoy my blackened salmon, and it was true that I felt better mentally and physically with food in my belly. Harvey had put away another burger—the man did love his red meat—while Sophie was picking through a salad. I asked the server to take my empty plate and turned to Harvey with the request that he dig into his wallet.

He produced an interesting assortment—two credit cards, issued by Cabela's and Outdoor World, six different airline frequent flyer cards, his membership card in the Sun Devils booster club, voter registration, car insurance, Medicare, another health insurance ID, and the driver's license. The street address was the same on each of those cards that carried this information, a street called Fairway Drive in Surprise, Arizona.

Where on earth was Surprise, Arizona?

I must have voiced the question aloud. Sophie piped up with, "West Valley." Harvey merely waved an arm in a gesture that might have been aiming west. I had no idea. I picked up my phone and keyed in his address. From my current location, holy yikes! It was *way* out there. The helpful little map information told me, in current traffic conditions it would take two hours and four minutes to drive there.

A four hour round trip, on top of everywhere else I'd been today, after my 4:19 a.m. awakening. No way. I needed to deliver Sophie home first if I was going to head west yet tonight.

"That address isn't current," Harvey informed me.

"Okay, what's your new one?"

His shoulders slumped. "I can't remember. Jeannie and I had moved to an assisted living place, a nice apartment, right before she had her stroke and had to go into that nursing home."

"Is the apartment in Surprise?"

His gaze went upward as he thought about that. "It's not that far from our old neighborhood, but the address … I think it's in Glendale."

Not that far from the old neighborhood pretty well cinched it for me, as far as driving out there tonight.

"Harvey, think very carefully about this. Who would know your new address? You said you didn't have kids, but is there a niece or nephew? Siblings of yours or Jeannie's? Neighbors or good friends?"

His expression didn't change as I mentioned nieces or nephews. With siblings and friends, he seemed sad. At his age, I'm sure many of them were gone already.

"We need to reach someone who knows where Jeannie is, preferably someone who could meet us here in Mesa and take you home. Can I see your phone?"

He handed it over and I went to his contacts list. There were fewer than a dozen, all listed simply by first names. I began reading them off to him.

"Barry? Who's that?"

"Oh, he's my hunting buddy. We used to get us an elk license every year, had the best time camping in this beat up old motorhome of his. Barry, he could always take a good elk."

"We could call him. He surely knows where you're living now."

Harvey shook his head. "He passed, more than two years ago. I just didn't have the heart to take his name off my list."

Similar responses came to each of the names. He remembered good times with these friends, but most were gone. A couple of them hadn't been in touch in years. "When the Christmas cards quit coming, Jeannie always knew. Another old friend was gone now."

I realized I could probably call some type of social services agency and put both Harvey and Sophie into their care, force the authorities to sort it out. But when Harvey picked up his crumpled paper napkin and dabbed at his eyes, I knew I couldn't do that. This poor man. He would eventually remember something, give me some clue. Maybe a good night's sleep would help to clarify his thought processes. If that didn't happen by morning, I could rethink the decision.

"Okay. We tried." I turned to Sophie. "Anything from your mom yet?"

She shook her head. "I should have got that tracker app so I could find out where her phone is."

Normally, I'd be horrified at the idea of someone being able to track another person so easily, but I had to admit in this case it would come in handy. Didn't matter—we didn't have it. To make us all feel better, I ordered a decadent dessert and three forks. It helped.

"Let's go back to your house, Sophie. Your mom will be home now. She's just not answering her phone because the battery died." If I repeated it to myself a few times, I might actually believe it.

But when we pulled up in front of the house, it was completely dark and closed up. At seven p.m. every other house on the block was brightly lit and full of activity. Okay, so much for positive thinking.

I looked up nearby hotels and found one about fifteen minutes away. For good measure I called to be certain they had two rooms available; with Thanksgiving weekend approaching, we couldn't take anything for granted. Harvey pulled out his credit card to cover his room, I paid for one for us girls, and we rode the elevator to the second floor, Harvey with his bowling bag, Sophie and her huge backpack, and me with a duffle full of heavy-duty winter clothing that would do me no good here where the temperature was still 73, even after dark.

In our room, Sophie and I put our phones on their chargers, took turns at the shower (where I rinsed out my two-day-old undies and hung them to dry). If this adventure continued much longer, I would need a quick stop at a Walmart to replenish with a minimum of underwear and a couple new shirts. By the time I walked out of the bathroom, Sophie was sprawled across her bed, completely out of it.

I pulled the duvet over her and felt a pang of sympathy. What must it feel like to return home, believing your mom would be eager to see you, only to find no one home and phone communication sketchy? Poor kid.

Poor Harvey.
Poor me.

Chapter 13

Despite all the current turmoil, I slept like a rock. Part of it was pure physical exhaustion—hours in a car in heavy traffic will do that—and part was mental. With so many unanswered questions, my brain needed a recharge. I woke a little before seven, seeing faint light around the edge of the curtain.

Sophie was burrowed into the covers, still zonked.

I dressed and walked next door to tap lightly on Harvey's door. Less than ten seconds later, he opened it. I studied his face, hoping he'd had a memory breakthrough. He did recall me and most of the details from yesterday.

"Help me figure out this silly coffee maker and I'll fix us both a cup," he said.

I followed the simple 1-2-3 steps illustrated on the machine and started a cup brewing for him. "Don't worry about making one for me. I need to get Sophie up and moving. The hotel has free breakfast downstairs. You can either go ahead or wait for us girls."

He gave a warm smile. "I'll wait for you girls. My bag is already packed, and I'll be on my way to Jeannie pretty soon."

"You've remembered the name of the place?"

"Oh. No, I thought you'd found it."

My smile was probably sort of feeble, but I assured him I was trying. While I waited for Sophie to dress and gather her things—it's amazing how much a teen can spread out in a hotel room, in just a few hours—I did a search for nursing care facilities, narrowing it down to the two cities Harvey had mentioned last night. There were dozens. The whole Phoenix area was a haven for the elderly, it seemed, especially the west side where the original Sun City started this trend. I could understand Harvey's confusion. Too many of the names included *desert, sunrise, sunset, oasis,* or *garden* in the name. How could anyone keep them straight? I began tapping locations and calling them.

Responses varied from "we don't give out patient information" to "a relative will need to come personally to make that inquiry." I refined my spiel to include the fact that I was with the patient's husband but he could not remember the name of the facility. He was desperately trying to find his wife. That garnered more sympathy but the person at the other end still usually wanted to talk to Harvey. After a few tries I realized I was spinning my wheels unless I had him with me. We could tackle this again over breakfast.

"I heard from my mom," Sophie announced. "She texted that she'll meet me at the house at noon. I could go there now. I'd be fine for a few hours until she gets there."

"Can I see the text?"

Eddie was going to meet you but forgot you'd be home today. Sorry. I'll be there by noon.

It had come in at 9:37 last night. Not an unreasonable hour at all, but something felt off. Why hadn't Dixie simply called? She'd agreed to be there, and now she was somewhere else and leaving Eddie to welcome her daughter home? Sophie could have put me on the line and I would have clarified a lot more facts about this plan. I handed her phone back and reminded myself to stop obsessing about details. People did things differently than I would, that's all.

"How will you get in?"

Her eye held a gleam. "Remember, I told you about my bedroom window …"

"We'll wait for your mom."

"No! I can get inside and I want to be home."

"You need me to drive you there."

"I have Uber and my mom's credit card all set up."

I wanted to tell her she wouldn't get away with it, but in reality all she had to do was leave my sight for five minutes. She'd grab her pack—or simply abandon it—run a few blocks in any direction and call for a ride. I could catch up with her at the house, but by then she'd probably have locked herself inside and escalated this into a big battle. I held more power if I simply went along with her idea.

"Okay, you win. Let's get breakfast here. Harvey's waiting for us. Then I'll drive you to your house."

It was probably the mention of Harvey that changed her mind. She'd obviously developed a fondness for the grandfatherly old man.

The two of them helped themselves at the breakfast bar while I brought up the list of nursing homes I'd previously been working on. I set my phone down and told Harvey to look through the names while I made myself a waffle and scooped fruit onto it. When I returned to the table, he was shaking his head.

"None of those you called seem familiar. Maybe this other one?" He pointed to a name and I clicked it to go to the website. But the photo of the building elicited another negative. "Nope. It's not a three-story place. Everything's on the ground level."

"That's helpful to know. We can eliminate some of the choices." Between bites of waffle, I started a systematic search.

Within the hour, we had three places that could be possibilities. I found myself getting almost excited. I could leave Sophie at her house, *if* we managed to connect a call to Dixie and I made absolutely certain the woman would be there for her daughter within a short time. Then I would deliver Harvey to his wife. And I might actually be on the road for Holbrook before noon, switch vehicles back to Ron's Mustang, and arrive home before bedtime tonight. Yes, I realized there were a lot of *ifs* in that plan, and things would need to go almost perfectly.

One could dream.

Chapter 14

Harvey and I followed Sophie into her back yard and watched her take the screen off the bedroom window. She pressed both palms to the glass, jiggled it, and the flimsy latch shifted just enough to allow the pane to slide open.

"You're pretty good at that, kid. When I was a boy, our windows had those cranks that went round and round. I had to use a prying technique to get mine open."

She sent a wink over her shoulder.

"Sophie, I'm going to be at the front door. You walk straight through the house and let us in. You don't get your pack until I make sure I'm leaving you in a safe situation."

Harvey had received a wink. I got an eye-rolling *whatever*. Why did I suddenly seem like the curmudgeon here? I'm young … I'm cool … really, I am. I sneaked in and out of my bedroom, maybe once.

I watched Sophie disappear into the house and I hightailed it to the front door. She opened it just as I got there.

"Everything look okay?" I asked.

"Yeah, pretty normal. It's weird, after being gone a few months. Guess Mom hasn't taken the trash out in a while—something stinks."

Harvey caught up and we both walked in. There was barely an entryway; we stepped directly into a fairly large living room with a fireplace and big sectional couch. A vase of daisies sat on a side table, the water evaporated and the flowers drooping. A dining room was to our left, the edge of a kitchen counter visible ahead, and a sliding glass door led to the back yard and patio. I could see a casserole dish on the counter, showing what looked like the burnt edges of something from a few days ago. Dixie's story of having just popped out for some shopping seemed to be crumbling by the minute.

"Whoo, smells like a dead thing!" Harvey commented.

"I'm getting rid of that trash bag," Sophie said, heading for the kitchen.

I'd noticed the smell, too, but it didn't seem polite to exclaim over it. That all changed approximately two seconds later when Sophie screamed. Something clattered to the floor and she came running toward us, a look of sheer panic on her face.

Harvey instinctively stretched his arms out and pulled her toward him. "Honey, honey, what's the matter?"

"Eddie—he's—" She couldn't get words out, only a flailing gesture toward the kitchen.

I stepped to the end of the counter. Yep, there was a

dead guy, sprawled on the floor with a huge chef's knife sticking out of his gut. Two black flies were buzzing over the pool of blood that surrounded him. I backed away, then turned to flee. In all my encounters with crime, I rarely saw a body up close. This was no time to make an exception.

"We gotta get out of here. Now!" I curved my arms outward, ushering them both toward the open front door.

Sophie's sobs had turned into hiccups. Harvey looked as though he was tempted to go back inside and get a good look.

"Huh-uh," I said. "It's very obviously a crime scene." Suicide by a knife to one's own heart isn't terribly common, despite that depiction in cinematic drama. "I'm calling the police, and we'll have to be here to tell them how we found him."

Our statements would have to include the admission of breaking and entering, but since Sophie's full handprints were clearly on the bedroom window, they should be able to verify our story without question.

I phoned 9-1-1. Harvey had an arm around Sophie, patting her shoulder. The girl was shaking pretty violently, but I couldn't think what to do for her at the moment other than offer a bottle of water I'd purchased yesterday. I went to the Highlander to get it.

She looked up, her eyes darting wildly between Harvey and me, as she reached for the water bottle. "I'm so scared, Charlie. Where's my mom?"

At that moment, two City of Mesa cruisers roared around the corner, lights strobing. Thankfully, no sirens. I imagined the officers would soon be asking the very same question about Dixie's whereabouts. As it turned out, the tough questions would come from the plainclothes detective who arrived in a white sedan a minute later. While the uniformed officers threaded yellow tape around the perimeter of the property and neighbors began to emerge from nearby houses, he walked over to us and introduced himself as Detective Hernandez.

Hernandez was tall, of slender build, with dark hair and a trim goatee. His tweed jacket fit well and his shoes were polished. His partner emerged from the sedan, a short woman with blonde hair, whose open jacket clearly revealed she was pregnant. She sent a weary smile toward Sophie.

The next couple of hours became a blur. I presented my ID and explained how I happened to be here with a teen girl and an elderly man who were unrelated to me. The answers seemed to satisfy. Harvey, likewise, was quickly dismissed when his muddled story and my corroboration convinced them he'd been nowhere near here, in fact had not even seen the body.

Sophie, being the one who could positively identify Eddie, took the brunt of the questioning. After she told them how we'd entered the house and described finding the victim on the kitchen floor, I finally stepped in and reminded them that I could vouch for Sophie's whereabouts for the past two and a half days, and that she really should not be questioned without the presence of a lawyer, her mother, or a social worker—or all three.

Which, of course, brought the detectives' full attention to the question of where Dixie O'Connell was at this moment. And none of us could answer that one.

"I don't *know* …" Sophie said, through tears. "We texted some and I talked to her once, yesterday. But I thought she was going to be home when we got here …"

I reached for the girl's hand and gave a little squeeze, warning her not to volunteer information. I could see this inquiry leading down a rabbit hole, with Dixie soon becoming the prime suspect. And for all I knew, the woman had grown desperate to get rid of Eddie. Sophie had told me about their arguments, how her mom wanted out of the relationship but the boyfriend wouldn't leave. I knew nothing about Dixie as a person, and had gotten mixed signals about her from her own daughter.

The one thing I could see clearly was that Sophie didn't believe her mom to be a killer, and the poor girl who'd lost her dad at a young age was possibly going to lose her other parent too. And the kid was scared. Really scared.

Considering a day ago I couldn't wait to get this teen girl off my hands, now I couldn't bring myself to simply drive away and leave her in the hands of a social worker and the system. She needed help.

And I needed some advice on how to handle this. I meandered over to the Highlander and leaned against it to make a call. A chilly breeze blew down the street and I grabbed for my lightweight fleece jacket.

Chapter 15

After yesterday's drive back from up north, Gracie Nelson had promised her kids pancakes and a lazy sleep-in Saturday. She was in the process of loading the dishwasher with syrupy plates when she saw Charlie Parker's name on her phone's screen. She took the incoming call right away.

"Hey, Charlie, what's new?" A moment later, "Oh my god …"

"I don't know if the police are planning to take Sophie into custody. They haven't said. I mean, she couldn't have killed Eddie—her alibi is easy enough to establish. But the kid needs support of some kind, an advocate, at the very least. I think Pen mentioned having connections …"

"Of course, of course. I'll get hold of her. Our friend Sandy lives in Mesa. Maybe it's best if I send her over right away. We can see where it goes from there."

Charlie thanked her and ended the call. Wow. Edward Peppard dead. Gracie switched off the burner under the kettle she'd filled, aiming for a leisurely cup of tea now that the kids had headed out to do their own things. So much for that plan. She speed-dialed Sandy and added Pen and Mary to the call, then went through the same quick rundown of events Charlie had just relayed to her.

"Oh my gosh, what if Linda …" Sandy's voice was strained.

"Don't go there. Not yet anyway," Pen said. "Of course we shall need to reach out to her, find out where she has been these past few days, establish that she could not have somehow tracked Edward to his current girlfriend's home."

"That's what the police will think," Mary added. "If the new girlfriend—I think you'd said her name is Dixie? If she has a solid alibi, the cops will start looking for other connections right away."

"For the moment," Gracie told them, "Charlie could use some help and support for this teen who is caught in the middle. Sandy, can you go over there and meet them, see what's up? And Pen, could Benton put some feelers out to see where the legal side of it goes? Charlie felt sure it was murder, but we won't know anything about the investigation unless we learn some inside information."

"Certainly."

"Absolutely," Sandy said. "I'm grabbing my bag and my jacket right now. Give me the address."

Gracie read from the note she'd jotted during Charlie's call. "Mary, can you reach out to Amber? I can't remember what time zone she's in now. Once you speak with her, see if she can tell us anything new about Linda's accounts— the ones Edward had access to."

"I'm on it." Their super-fit team member, Mary, was the one who'd been ready to dash out and kick Eddie Peppard's rear when they first learned how he'd been using their friend Linda.

Now, Gracie was glad none of them had personally approached the man. She glanced at her phone screen. Sandy and Mary had left the call but Pen was still there.

"Pen, remind me … when we were talking to Charlie and Sophie at that little café in Holbrook, I made some kind of rash statement about wishing Edward Peppard was gone from the face of the earth, didn't I? Did I actually say I wished him dead? Will Charlie remember that?"

Pen chuckled. "I don't think you went quite that far, love. Certainly you couldn't be considered a suspect, and Charlie definitely doesn't seem the type to throw you under the bus in that manner."

Gracie gave a nervous laugh. Pen was right. Charlie seemed like a very stand-up person; she wouldn't incriminate someone she'd hardly met in order to save this teenager. But what about Sophie? She'd been there during the conversation and if her mother became the main suspect, a desperate daughter might do just about anything.

A desperate daughter. Gracie froze in the middle of wiping down her kitchen counter. She remembered the first time she'd met Pen's friend, Linda Ratcliff. Linda's daughter had called upon her old friend for help. Linda's life savings were in jeopardy, but it was Rosalie who'd been at her wit's end. Gracie remembered the conversation in detail.

Pen had called a meeting of the Heist Ladies at her Scottsdale home with its up-close view of Camelback Mountain. When Gracie walked in, the first of the friends to arrive, she quickly picked up on the level of stress in the room. Pen introduced her friend, Linda Ratcliff, whom she'd known for decades.

Like Pen, Linda was a classic beauty. That day she'd worn tailored black slacks and a red cashmere sweater—expensive but understated. Her dark hair was going silver, with a dramatic swath swooping down across her right cheek, the left side tucked behind her ear. Gracie would have guessed her to be in her mid-seventies, although Pen had recently told her Linda had celebrated her eighty-first birthday. Linda had greeted her quietly, with sad amber eyes.

Pen then introduced Linda's daughter, Rosalie, and Gracie quickly picked up the anxiety coming from the younger woman, practically in waves. She was a carbon copy of her mother, twenty-five years younger. Except where there was sadness on Linda's face, Rosalie's was etched with worry. Haggard lines around her mouth showed exhaustion; her entire demeanor was that of hopelessness.

Pen offered tea, and while she organized cups and the teapot, Sandy and Mary arrived. Introductions all around, and Amber, now working from Spain, was brought in via a video chat on Pen's iPad.

"Now that we're all here," Pen began, "I shall let Linda and Rosalie tell their story and why they've requested our help."

Linda took the delicate cup and saucer Pen offered, holding them on her lap as she spoke. "I had the best marriage in the world," she said. "Roger and I were simpatico in almost everything, especially in our love of travel. Once he retired from the world of finance, we booked one trip after the other. We hit every continent and a big percentage of the countries. When he passed, five years ago—" The cup rattled and she sniffled.

Rosalie took up the story. "Mother just needed a companion. We knew that no one would ever replace Daddy, but we all—my two siblings and I—understood that Mother still had a lot of life ahead of her and wanted someone at her side."

Some kind of look passed between the two, a silent go-ahead for Rosalie to continue.

"Just at a year after Daddy's death, Mother met Edward Peppard. There was a mutual acquaintance … the impression was given that Edward had known this circle of friends for years. It felt safe. None of us thought to ask a lot of questions."

"Even I didn't question," Linda added. "When Edward talked about mutual friends, events we'd both attended, I assumed I actually had met him previously, I just didn't recall the specifics. He was charming, gentlemanly, and we had the same taste in theater and classical music. I'd long dreamed of traveling to Alaska, making a long road trip of it, but of course that was a bit beyond what a woman my age should be doing on her own. Edward put everything else aside so he could take me. We loaded up his truck and had the most wonderful month. He declared his love for me, told me he'd go to the ends of the earth for me. Of course, the feeling wasn't mutual—I would never stop loving Roger—but Edward was great fun. I needed some fun in my life about that time." She glanced back at her daughter.

"None of us questioned any details or thought to do a background check on the man. He made Mother happy and that was a relief. They were always on the go."

"What changed?" Pen asked gently.

Rosalie was the first to answer. "About a year ago, I learned how much Mother's finances had become tied up with Edward's. Or, I should say, how little he was actually contributing. We'd heard that he owned a home, up near Flagstaff somewhere, and he derived rental income from that, and he had a pension. But the only thing he seemed to pay for were drinks with friends. All the everyday expenses, from food to clothing to travel to maintenance on the home, was paid for on a credit card in my mother's name. He carried a card on that account and used it quite freely."

"It was a mutual agreement," Linda inserted. "I didn't mind. I had plenty. Roger left me quite well off, and why not spend some of that to enjoy my senior years."

"No one was arguing about that—any of it. My sister confided that she believed Edward was a gold-digger, but we all kept our mouths shut because Mother was enjoying her life."

Pen nudged once more. "But something is different now?"

"About a month ago, Mother wanted to make a change to her trust documents, and she asked me to attend a meeting with her attorney because I've been named as her successor trustee. That part was all set up during my father's time."

Sandy, the banker, was nodding.

"During the meeting with the lawyer, I learned that Mother had made a previous change I didn't know about, giving Edward a lifetime interest in our family home. He could live there the rest of his days, and he was given many other privileges with the property, such as being allowed to remodel or lease it to someone else. All the furnishings and family heirlooms were to stay. I was surprised and somewhat dismayed. Previously, the home we grew up in was understood to belong to the siblings. If no one wanted to live there, it would be sold and added to Mother's estate. It's a sizeable property, with a value of more than three million dollars."

"Your attorney went along with this change?" Sandy asked, a bit sharply.

"He wasn't happy about it," Linda admitted. "He'd told me the scenario could become a nightmare. That was the reason for the meeting last month. I wanted Rosalie to know my wishes and to be included in the discussion."

"The attorney stayed with his point, that the entire estate would be tied up for the rest of Edward's life. As personal representative and trustee, I wouldn't be able to do anything with that property for years to come."

Gracie saw the haggard expression return to Rosalie's face.

"The result of the meeting was that the law firm is to draw up new documents, taking ownership of any of Mother's assets away from Edward, leaving him with a decent cash settlement instead."

"Which sounds very generous, considering everything your mother has already paid for," Mary said.

"Exactly. I began going through all of Mother's paperwork, studying investment accounts and bank statements, and I discovered that everything Edward had access to had suddenly vanished. It was fairly elaborate. He held two joint credit cards with her, plus a joint checking account and one investment account in his own name at a major brokerage firm. Money from Mother's investments held at this same firm had been transferred into his account and then moved to another place Mother knew nothing about. Large purchases on the credit card were automatically paid from her account. I came to discover gambling debts at several casinos, both in this area and out of state, and there were travel expenses I didn't recognize, short trips to Vegas, signs there could be another woman."

Linda had set her tea aside, untouched, and was practically crying now. "I was such a fool, never looking at my account statements closely. Edward assured me he was checking everything. All the bills were getting paid on time, and I was happy just to travel and not worry about anything."

"Little did she know, her investment accounts which had totaled in the range of four to five million now contained just a few thousand dollars. The credit card bills were accumulating at a rate where her remaining account balances would have been completely cleared out within a few more weeks."

Sandy looked horrified. "What steps have you taken?"

Rosalie took a deep breath. "I alerted the investment firm, changed all her passwords, and had the credit agencies freeze her accounts. The lawyer is in the process of getting her will and trust documents updated, but these guys work *so* slowly. Weeks have slipped by, and we're—"

Linda placed a hand on her daughter's knee. "I can say it." She looked around the room at the Ladies. "I'm dying. Last week, I was hospitalized for several days and the tests did not bring good news. I wanted my children to receive my estate. Roger would have been so disappointed in me. I—"

"I want to get her money back." Rosalie was adamant. "The man is a con artist, a gold-digger, whatever you want to call him, but this is wrong on every level. All of my father's hard work and judicious investing cannot go to this ... this ... scumbag."

Gracie felt anger rise and saw eyes flashing on all the other faces in the room. On the video chat, Amber appeared to be tapping keys on a keyboard. "Send me more information on this guy, whatever you have, and I'll see what I can track."

"Our young computer genius," Pen said with a smile.

"Where is Edward now?" Mary asked. "Surely he's not still living in your home?"

"Vanished," Linda said. "The day Rosalie and I returned from the attorney appointment, he wasn't at home. I thought he was simply out somewhere, but I checked the safe. His passport and important documents are gone. I fear he could easily leave the country."

Rosalie turned to the group, keeping her voice low. "This man has upended our lives. Mother is devastated that he's not who he represented himself to be, and of course I'm livid at what he's gotten away with. I hate what he's done to her, and if I could catch up with the man, I'd kill him."

Linda registered no surprise. "Sweetie, you're the one with everything to lose. I would need to do it."

Those words echoed in Gracie's head now, as she put away the pancake mix and syrup and headed out the door to join Charlie and Sophie in Mesa. What if one of the Ratcliff women truly had followed through?

Chapter 16

I liked Sandy Werner as soon as she walked over and introduced herself to Sophie and me. A banker, she and I both spoke the language of accounting and finance. She was slightly older than I, a little on the plump side, with a flattering blonde pageboy cut and vivid blue eyes. She said Gracie and Pen were on their way from other parts of the metro area. And there was Gracie, parking a couple houses down the street, just as Sandy said it.

Detective Hernandez approached, eyeing our growing little group. "We're taking the girl downtown. She's not a suspect at this point. Her alibi checks out with the social services people in Santa Fe, but she's here as a minor without next of kin to claim her. Until her mother comes along, she needs to be in the system here."

Gracie spoke up, reaching for Sophie's hand,

introducing herself to the detective and his partner. "This poor kid's been through a lot, going on for months now. I'd be happy to take her into my own household until her mother comes back."

"Sophie has heard from her mom within the past twenty-four hours. It won't be long before Dixie gets back," I offered.

"Procedure. You're welcome to come downtown, talk with the social worker in our department, and present your credentials. I'm not saying it won't work out for you to go with this lady," he said to Sophie, "but we have rules to follow."

"So, is this where my responsibility ends?" I asked, a little uncertain about simply driving away.

"As far as the girl's custody, yes. As far is being a person who discovered a murder victim … we'd like you to stay here in the metro area a couple more days. Questions are going to come up."

It wasn't really what I wanted to hear. Getting home had been my top priority and the trip had already dragged on far longer than I wanted. But now that there was a mystery to solve …

"You're certainly welcome to stay with me," Sandy said. "Unless you're allergic to cats."

"Um, I don't think I am. I've always had dogs." Then I remembered Harvey, who was now sitting in the front passenger seat of my rental. "I've got another delivery before I can make any firm plans."

We retrieved Sophie's pack from the back of the Highlander and I watched, a little wistfully, as the female officer escorted her to a cruiser. I noticed a similar expression on Gracie's face.

"Sophie told me she thought you'd be a great mom," I said. "She liked the fact that you set boundaries with your own kids."

Gracie smiled at the compliment. "Oh, I don't know. I just do my best." She paused a second. "Maybe it says something about the situation in Sophie's home, though. Kind of sad, huh."

"Anyone hungry? It's almost twelve," Harvey said.

Gracie shrugged. "I just finished pancakes at home."

I hadn't eaten much at breakfast, and Sandy suggested a restaurant would be a better place for us to discuss Eddie Peppard than here at the scene where a coroner's vehicle had just backed into the driveway in preparation for hauling him away. She got the word out to Pen and their other colleague, Mary, whom I hadn't met yet. We all headed for a Chinese buffet that was about ten minutes away on Power Road.

"What's the story with the elderly gentleman?" Mary asked, as soon as she and I were alone.

I liked the athletic woman with her short, spiky hair and can-do attitude. Gracie had briefly mentioned that she'd met Mary when the woman was down on her luck. You wouldn't know it to look at her now. She and I had offered to hold a table while the others helped themselves to the array of fantastic-smelling dishes.

I gave the short version of how Harvey had tagged along with us and now couldn't remember the name or address of where his wife was staying.

"Ooh, that's rough. For both of you."

The others returned to the table, Mary and I took our turns at the buffet, and at last conversation resumed around the death of Eddie Peppard.

"Have you informed Linda yet?" I asked Pen.

The classy older woman shook her head. "It's something best delivered in person, I think. Linda's not well, and although I believe the news will come as a relief, there will be many unanswered questions. I'd like her daughter Rosalie to be there."

"Rosalie is administering her mother's affairs and will be trustee for her estate," Sandy said. "If Edward Peppard had started playing the same games with Dixie that he was with Linda—"

She stopped short of any accusation, but I mentally filled in the blanks. Gracie had dropped small hints about Eddie's scamming their friend for millions of dollars, which could make for a very worthy motive for murder. None of them wanted to think of Linda or Rosalie as killers.

Dixie was now his latest victim. And Dixie was conveniently out of sight. The thoughts I'd refused to voice in front of Sophie were now facing me head-on.

"The mother may not be the murderer," Gracie said now, as if she'd read my mind. "She could very well be another victim of this Eddie guy." She picked up a spring roll and dunked it in sauce.

"Indeed. It sounds as if she is, at least in the financial realm," Pen added. "It's exactly what happened to Linda."

"Agreed. I'd heard that Sophie's father left Dixie financially comfortable when he died. And that seemed to be Eddie's method, to find women with substantial means and figure out how to live off of them."

Harvey had been fiddling with chopsticks, I noticed, but he finally gave them up in favor of a fork. "Well, nobody's going to live off my fortune but a bunch of pampered pups at the humane society," he announced, as he stabbed a shrimp. "Jeannie and I already got that set up. Course, who knows how much will be left after both of us finish out our lives at Desert Rose."

"Harvey—you said Desert Rose. Is that the place?" I wiped my hands on my napkin and picked up my phone.

A quick search for Desert Rose, paired with *nursing*, gave me a name and address. I tapped to access their website and up came photos of a sprawling facility amid palm trees and flowering bougainvillea. Pinkish stucco and turquoise trim on the doors gave it a distinctive look. I aimed my phone's screen toward him and he lit up, nodding vigorously.

"That's it. I knew it."

"Let me just call and make sure. Then we can head over there after lunch."

"I'll be back with Jeannie in time for dinner. They make real good dinners there." He squared his shoulders and sat up straighter, happy at last.

"What will you do after you take Harvey home?" Mary asked.

"I guess I'll drive back to this side of town. Detective Hernandez said I needed to stay in the area a couple more days. I'd like to see Sophie reunited with her mom, since that was my original assignment. At the very least, I can't just go away and leave the girl in state custody and the mother's fate completely unknown."

"You'll want to head over to Surprise fairly soon," Sandy advised. "After three p.m. the traffic is murder, and you'll face a lot less of it if you're back in Mesa before then."

"Good idea." I glanced over at Harvey. With the good news that he was going home, the man was shoveling chow mein like his life depended on it. His plate was nearly clean.

I finished my last bites of sweet and sour pork and took a moment to savor the green tea in my cup. While Harvey made a trip to the boy's room (I swear, the man must have a bladder the size of a pinto bean), I consulted map directions and figured out that I-10 would deliver us to the west side by the quickest means. I memorized the exit names and the address of our destination.

Contact details for Pen and Gracie were already in my phone, and I quickly added those for Sandy and Mary.

"Call me when you get back to Mesa," Sandy said. "I'll have my guest room ready for you."

"If I've heard from my friend Benton by then, we may have more details about the Edward Peppard mess," Pen added.

I met my 92-year-old charge at the exit, and we walked out to the SUV. Making certain his bowling bag luggage was still with us, we headed for the Loop 202 and then Interstate 10. Nothing in my experience of driving in Albuquerque prepared me for the organized manner in which the Phoenix designers move a massive amount of traffic around this huge metro area. The drivers were no less obnoxious, but at least the eight lanes moved steadily.

An hour later, we pulled up at Desert Rose Life Care. A smaller sign beside the entry drive stated that it was a home for assisted living and all levels of later-life care.

"Right over there is where I always park," Harvey said, directing me toward the left side of the main building. "Our apartment is in this section."

I parked and we walked through the main entrance, into a lobby that resembled a fine hotel with Queen Anne chairs upholstered in floral fabrics and a reception desk of cherry.

"Mr. Molson, it's good to see you back," said the middle-aged woman behind the desk. "How was your trip?"

"Wait'll I tell you," he said with a grin.

"Is this your daughter?"

He shook his head. "She's what you'd call a friend in need. My car disappeared. Charlie brought me right home."

Even though it hadn't been quite that simple, I appreciated the brevity of his story. I didn't know whether to offer more explanation or just let it go. He should file a claim with his insurance company and probably report it to the police, but I figured that was his business.

"Will you be okay now?" I asked. A glance toward the woman behind the desk, and her nod reassured me.

Harvey set down his bowling bag then reached out and took both of my hands in his. "Thank you, Charlie. It's been a great adventure and I enjoyed the pleasure of your company."

Aww, what a sweetie. Our couple of days together had been frustrating at times, and I still wondered whether he truly had forgotten the name of Desert Rose or if he really just wanted to tag along for a new experience.

He leaned forward and placed a kiss on my cheek.

Chapter 17

I was most of the way back to Mesa when I realized I was about to be someone's house guest and all I had with me were winter clothes and a toothbrush. At minimum, a change into fresh jeans and a new shirt really were in order. I spotted a Walmart store, took the next exit, and found my way to it.

In the parking lot, it occurred to me this might be the only time I'd be alone for a while, so I gave Drake a quick call and explained the situation.

"Just be careful," he said, his usual response whenever I find myself tied up in something unforeseen.

"I'm hoping the authorities have already located Sophie's mother and the two can be reunited. But it's a little complicated in that regard. At least you don't have to worry about me bringing a kid home with me—someone else already has dibs on her."

Next up was a call to Josh at the lot where I'd rented the Highlander. Didn't want him thinking I'd taken off with it. No worries. As long as the Mustang was in Tyler's garage, he knew I'd be back.

Ron was a little less happy to hear that I still didn't have his car. But when I suggested he could drive to Holbrook himself and leave my Jeep for me to pick up later, he backed down. Turned out Albuquerque had received some snow and he was content to have the four-wheel-drive instead of his Mustang. He asked if I'd be home for Thanksgiving.

Oh. A holiday weekend was coming soon and I'd made no plans. But I couldn't exactly promise anything. I told him to be sure Gram and Dottie were invited to his house that day, even if I wasn't home yet.

With things at home taken care of, I trotted into Walmart and went on a little shopping spree. A small wheeled suitcase held the two pairs of jeans, three pullover shirts, a nightshirt, a pack of socks, pack of undies, and assorted toiletries that would get me through the basics of shampooing and cleaning up well enough to be around other people for a few more days. I tossed in a pair of nicer slacks, some black flats, and a dressier sweater, for just in case. What if the police wanted me to stay through the Thanksgiving weekend? I really didn't want to contemplate it, but it was better to be ready.

I followed Sandy's directions to her home, which I found to be a one-story brick house in a neighborhood where all the others were stucco. An inflatable turkey sat in the yard. As she'd told me, it was easy to spot. The front porch sported pumpkins, autumn leaves, and a rocking chair with cushions in fall colors. It was a little frou-frou for my taste, but from the little bit I'd seen of Sandy, I guessed it reflected her personality well.

She'd apparently spotted me through the wide mullioned window at the front because the door opened as I approached.

"Welcome! Come on in." She introduced me to Heckle and Jeckle, her two black cats. After suspicious sniffs at my new luggage, they proceeded to ignore me. "Pen will be here in a few minutes, so let me show you to the guestroom first."

The feminine touches everywhere attested to the fact that she lived alone. Pastel tones, flowered wallpaper, and dozens of little figurines and painted plates decorated nearly every surface. My room turned out to be something out of a B&B dream—four-poster bed, carved oak dresser, pillows and comforters all over the place. Complete with the adjoining bathroom, I must say, I certainly couldn't have gotten any better surroundings in an upscale hotel.

I unwrapped my new packets of blusher, lip balm, and sunscreen and set my shampoo and conditioner beside the shower. Then I cut the tags off the new clothes, hanging everything in the closet to get the wrinkles to relax a bit. Sandy's guest room—like any fine hotel—provided an ironing board and iron tucked away in the closet, for that purpose, but ironing is kind of on my I-don't-do-that list.

Properly settled, I walked back to the living room to discover that Pen had arrived. A china tea service sat on a silver tray on the coffee table, and the two women were chatting. Sandy spotted me and offered a cup.

"It's a good Assam," she said. "It'll perk you up after the long drive across the city."

I had to admit that it was hard to believe I'd made a hundred-forty mile round trip without leaving the massive metroplex. "At least it looks like Harvey is settled. I didn't meet his wife, but the lady in charge was all set to take over and get him to Jeannie's room."

Sandy handed me a cup of the steaming tea and gestured toward the overstuffed chairs near the front window. "Pen has news."

"Well, not much, I'm afraid." Pen had perched on an upright Queen Anne chair, and she paused to take a quick sip of her tea. "I got in touch with Benton—that's my friend who retired from the district attorney's office. He's been of immense help to us in the past, as he still has loads of contacts on the law enforcement side of things."

Sandy held out a plate of homemade butter cookies and I took one.

"Benton tells me the word is they'll rush an autopsy on Edward Peppard's body because the initial observation was a bit unusual."

"Really? In what way, did he say?"

"It's unclear whether the knife wound was actually the cause of the man's death."

A picture flashed into my head. You don't quickly forget what a body with a knife in it looks like. I would have guessed the knife went straight to the heart.

"At any rate," she continued, "Benton will get back to me as he learns anything new. Meantime, they are of course looking for Dixie O'Connell as the chief suspect. He was in her kitchen, with one of her knives in him, and she hasn't been seen in several days."

"Did Benton have any information as to when the victim died?" I asked, picking crumbs of the butter cookie from my sweater.

"Nothing official. Again, the autopsy. But the initial

reading from the coroner placed it at least two days prior."

I pondered that, going back in time to Sophie's movements. She'd been with me since Thursday and in the custody of social services for several days before that. It definitely ruled her out as a suspect, but what about Dixie?

"Sophie *told* me she spoke and texted with her mother while we were on the road. But once we got here, she didn't seem surprised to find that Dixie wasn't home after all, and Sophie wanted to let herself into the house and stay alone."

"Clearly, she did not know there was a body in the kitchen."

"Obviously. But where did she think her mother was? Maybe Dixie told her something."

"Too bad the authorities have Sophie and her phone," Sandy mused.

"Did you get the idea Sophie was actually communicating with her mother?" Pen asked. "Thinking aloud here, I wonder if someone else might have possession of Dixie's phone?"

I'd had the same thought. "But that person would have most likely been Eddie, trying to hide something from the daughter if he'd placed her mom in jeopardy, don't you think? Plus, I did hear a female voice on the phone with Sophie at one point." I remembered during the call, thinking the voice sounded young, that Sophie and a friend might be messing with me. And then the call dropped.

"What if Dixie was at home, there was a confrontation with Eddie, and she killed him?"

"Good point, Sandy. And then most likely she would have run, needing to get away. What do you think, Charlie?"

"I'm not so sure. Unless Sophie was lying about the

content of the texts, her mom was telling her to come home. That she would be there. Then she backtracked. In fact, at one point she said she had to be away but Eddie would meet us—this was before he supposedly *forgot*. Still, it makes no sense that Dixie would send her daughter home if she knew he was dead inside the house."

"True." Pen set her cup aside, her forehead wrinkled thoughtfully. "It rules Dixie out as a suspect."

"Or … it means someone else had the mother's phone and was deliberately steering Sophie home, maybe in hopes that the girl would then become the most likely suspect." Sandy's suggestion might work.

"They had no way of knowing Sophie and I were running behind schedule because of the flat tire and car breakdown. If we'd actually arrived on the afternoon we were supposed to …"

We might have walked in just in time to see the killer leaving. But that sounded like the work of a master criminal, someone who planned the timing of their crime down to the second. Something about that scenario was just a little too pat.

"Going back to the idea that Eddie, or someone, had possession of Dixie's phone," Sandy said. "Couldn't it mean that Dixie is quite possibly a victim herself?"

"Or, in desperation, she killed Eddie and is now hiding out?"

I gave a sigh. "Desperation. That's probably a good word for it, Pen. If he was pulling the same scam on Dixie as he was with your friend Linda, I can see how she may have been desperate to get rid of him."

Sandy sat forward. "We should bring in Amber, see if she can learn more about Dixie's financial situation. Eddie was definitely after the money he could get from Linda. If Dixie had substantial means, she could have very well been his current target."

Chapter 18

From her work area, Amber Zeckis took a long look at the view of the spires atop the magnificent Catedral de Sevilla and the lovely fountain in the courtyard below her apartment, then initiated the video call to Sandy Werner in Mesa, Arizona. The eight-hour time difference always worked well for the Heist Ladies. When Sandy called after dinner in Arizona, night-owl Amber jumped online and spent a couple hours tracking down the information she wanted. Her VPN assured that the tracking links on various websites would register her searches as coming from within the US and not throw up any red flags.

"Hey, I hope 6 a.m. isn't too early for you," she said, noting that her friend's computer was obviously set up in the kitchen and Sandy was pulling a bagel from the toaster as she settled in for the call.

"Not a bit. Figured I'd grab some breakfast while we talk. I don't have to be at the bank until nine." She spread butter and jam on one half of the bread.

"I got hooked. Stayed online until nearly four this morning, but I managed some decent sleep. I'm actually having breakfast myself." She held up a small bowl, showing off her yogurt with blueberries.

"Find anything good? Maybe I should wake my houseguest and bring her in to hear this."

"No need," said a voice in the background. A woman with long hair pulled into a messy bun spoke to Sandy as she crossed the picture and reached for the coffee carafe. "I heard voices and smelled coffee."

"Amber, meet Charlie. Charlie, Amber." Sandy held up the unadorned half of her bagel, but Charlie shook her head. "Food later, coffee first. Hi, Amber. I've heard good things about you and your computer skills."

"Cool. I have to admit I didn't find a lot of detail on your Dixie O'Connell, but if you're ready for what I did find …"

"Go for it," Sandy said.

Charlie took a stool at the counter beside her, so they could both watch.

"So, on the face of it, Dixie doesn't seem wealthy. She's no socialite, for sure. Doesn't flaunt money. She's kind of a party girl, posts Insta pics of herself. Here's a few." Amber switched over to sharing her screen and showed some of the shots she'd captured.

Dixie looked enough like Sophie to be her older sister, and her youthful attitude came through in her saucy expression. Wearing a vest bedazzled with rhinestones and a bright pink cowboy hat, she grinned at the camera and raised a margarita glass. One would not peg her immediately as the mother of a teen. In other shots, she showed off red cowboy boots and short skirts. There were always friends and they were usually in a crowded bar scene.

"She dresses just like her kid. Maybe they share clothes. What does she do for a living?" Charlie asked. "Partying all the time doesn't come cheap. She has a nice little house, small but from my quick trip there it seemed well furnished, not at all run down. Whether she owns or rents, she's spent some money on the place."

Amber switched from the photos to another screen, a spreadsheet that was a bit too small to read at a distance. "Dixie doesn't work, actually has a trust fund."

"She's from a wealthy family?"

"As near as I can tell, the trust was set up by her husband. I don't know how their personalities meshed— maybe really well—but he knew his way around money and investments. He was a few years older, met Dixie when she was in high school, he in college. He went right to work for one of the big investment firms at a decent salary. She got pregnant and they married. She was able to stay home with the baby and he must have managed the money for them both. He tucked away a very nice portfolio and set it up so if anything happened to him the money would be paid out monthly rather than handing over a lump sum. The stocks throw off enough dividend income to support Dixie and Sophie without touching the principle, which is growing well as long as it's left alone."

Sandy was nodding. Charlie was chewing at her lower lip.

"My parents did a similar thing for me," Charlie said. "It's not move-to-the-Riviera wealth, but it covers the bills so I've never had to worry."

Sandy squinted at the numbers and pointed. "Yes, I can see how he did it. These are good, solid stocks, the kind that made Warren Buffet a wealthy man over time."

Amber pulled up another screenshot. "About six months ago, it looks like Dixie petitioned the court to make her the trustee so she could control the money herself. The request was denied on the basis that her husband had specifically stated that neither Dixie nor Sophie ever gain personal control. The trust department at the investment firm will always have full control. If they ever became insolvent—which is unlikely since they've been around since the 1920s—another financial institution takes over."

"So it sounds like he knew exactly what Dixie's actions would be. He set this up proactively so his earnings and investments wouldn't be squandered on partying and margaritas."

Sandy nodded at Charlie's comment, raised an index finger and added, "And men. We believe Edward Peppard entered her life less than a year ago. Based on our friend Linda's experience, I can easily see this Eddie pressing Dixie to quit bowing to the wishes of the bank and control her own money."

Amber took down the screen-share and picked up her bowl again. "That's a similar MO to what he used with Linda Ratcliff, right? Lonely widow, plenty of money."

"Dapper man comes in and shows her a good time, offers to take over the worrisome task of paying the bills and filing the taxes ... or whatever he did for her," Charlie added.

"His being a bit older than Dixie might have appealed to her. Being a lot younger than Linda definitely flattered her."

"Con men are always chameleons," Amber said. "We've learned that through every case we've worked on together, haven't we?"

"Indeed." Sandy had finished her bagel and set the plate aside. "They'd make fantastic actors because they are always playing the role, presenting the face that the target wants to see."

Charlie looked at her, realizing something. "I wonder if that's why both women admitted the guy would just take off from time to time, vanish for a day or two with plans of his own? Maybe maintaining the role constantly becomes a strain, requires the con artist to get away and regroup."

Now it was Sandy's turn to smile. "I hadn't thought of that. Linda did mention that Edward would be 'away on business' quite a bit."

"And Sophie told me she liked the times when Eddie left for a few days and it would just be her and her mom again."

Amber nodded. "Could also mean he was seeing one of them when he left the other … It's how men pull off the dual family routine."

"Wow." Charlie reached for the sack of bagels. "Okay, I've got just one more question before we sign off, Amber. How do you gather all this data on someone without them agreeing to a credit check?"

Amber smiled. "I'm just good with a computer. Sandy can tell you, I only ever check up on the bad guys we're investigating."

Chapter 19

Yes, she's quite the little computer whiz," Sandy told me as I put my bagel in the toaster. "As a banker, myself, I have to be careful how much I really know. There've been a couple of cases where the person we're investigating is a client of our bank. I can't get involved in that, obviously."

She put her plate in the dishwasher and offered me more coffee. "You asked some well-informed questions just now. What's your financial background?"

"Accountant." I went into the explanation about how Ron and I formed RJP Investigations and I was in charge of the finances. "My brother is the licensed investigator, but I somehow get dragged into that aspect of it at times too. Escorting Sophie home to Arizona was just a side gig, wasn't supposed to turn into all this."

"All of us, the Heist Ladies, had real lives with ordinary

days until we got together to help Pen recover a stolen necklace. She's a bestselling writer, you know."

"Pen? She doesn't talk about it much."

"No, she's scaled back on the book tours and such, but she still turns out a new book every year or two." She reached into the fridge. "I've got cream cheese if you want it. Or there's that homemade blackberry jam by the toaster."

I opted for the jam, as she had.

"I meant to ask Amber if she'd spotted any recent charges on Dixie's credit cards, any ATM withdrawals. I completely forgot."

"She did check that, said there was nothing within the past week. I guess I had covered that subject before you walked into the room."

"Okay, good. I mean, good that you asked. Not good that there's been no activity." I took a bite, savoring the sharp sweetness of the fresh fruit jam.

"I know. It doesn't seem likely that someone with Dixie's interests hasn't needed some money in recent days. If she hasn't been home, she's eating, drinking, and sleeping somewhere."

"We assumed with Eddie, until yesterday." Which reminded me that Dixie could very well be the killer. I was sure the police hoped the case would be solved so easily, but I couldn't help but feel for the thirteen-year-old who would lose her mom.

Sandy seemed to read my thoughts. "You'll want to stay in touch with Pen and see if she's picked up any new information. I'd better get dressed and turn my attention toward my real job."

She headed toward her bedroom and I finished my bagel. The two cats sat on the breakfast nook window seat, watching birds who visited a feeder as the sky grew lighter. Heckle and Jeckle spoke in tiny *mrow-mrow* sounds that must have been meant to entice the cardinals. Or maybe it was just a way of telling each other what their bird-catching strategy would be. Freckles would be eyeing the block of suet, wondering if it was as tasty as those odd creatures were making it out to be.

I joined the cats on the bench, pulling my nightshirt over my knees, and took a minute to check my messages and email. Nothing from Ron. "Love you and miss you" from Drake, with a selfie of him with Freckles. I felt a pang, missing them too. It would be Thanksgiving in a few days and I just wanted to be home.

It was a bit past seven-thirty. Would this be a decent hour to call Detective Hernandez?

Sandy bustled through the kitchen and into her walk-in pantry, her hair freshly brushed, makeup in place, and dressed now in a flattering blue suit with a coral-pink blouse. She scooped up cat food and divided it into two small bowls and checked their water dish. "Sorry to leave you on your own, but I know you've got plenty to do. There's a key on the hall table, so you can come and go. It's going to be a busy week at the bank, or I'd take the time off."

"No problem. I was just thinking about calling Pen. Is it too early?"

"Oh no, she's an early riser. Good idea—maybe she's heard something back from Benton." And with that she shrugged into her suit jacket and picked up her purse. The connecting door to the garage opened and closed, and I heard her car start.

Alone. In a city where I didn't really want to be, on

a case that had turned a simple road trip into a murder investigation. Ugh. Of course, I could defy the police and simply leave. The idea was *so* tempting. I wasn't sure what they could actually do to me, since I had no personal role in the case. Worst scenario, they could haul me back for questioning or make me pay a fine of some kind. Best scenario, they wouldn't do anything at all. They might even forget I existed.

Nah, that wasn't going to happen. Hernandez had a pretty stern look in his eye when he issued the order. And then there was Sophie. As self-centered and rude as she'd been in the beginning, the girl did have a vulnerable side.

All at once I saw myself, only two years older than Sophie's age now, orphaned, defiant, bratty. And Elsa, my gram, had been there for me. She could have said "sorry, not my kid" but she had taken me in and loved me, no matter what.

I swallowed hard and wiped away the tear that threatened to spill.

With a deep breath I made up my mind. I needed to follow this up and at least see if we could locate Sophie's mother.

I walked back to the guest room where I set out fresh clothes, showered, and treated myself to a thorough shampoo and conditioning routine. When I emerged and dressed, I saw that I had a voicemail. Talk about great timing.

"Charlie, it's Pen Fitzpatrick. I've got some new information from Benton. Call me when you're up."

So I did.

"I've spoken with Benton. It seems an autopsy was performed on Edward Peppard, rather late last night. It appears the knife was not the cause of death."

Someone else had said that and I'd forgotten to question. "How on earth could that be?" I still vividly remembered the knife in the center of the chest, the pool of blood, the very dead man.

"According to the medical examiner's preliminary report, which Benton saw because he and the man are golfing chums and he called in a favor, the most likely cause of death was a blow to the head."

Which also could have bled a lot. "So the knife wound was not in a location that would kill him?"

"Apparently it missed the central part of the heart, nicking only an edge. The blow to the head was far worse."

"You said this was a preliminary report?"

"Yes, so there are more tests to be done before the final ruling. Still, it's interesting don't you think?"

I agreed.

"Charlie, I've been told the police intend to keep all of this information away from the public. That means we cannot discuss it with anyone outside our small group."

"Understood. Since there are two very different wounds, I'm guessing they want to see what types of confessions come in. Sandy said the story was on the early news, identifying Edward Peppard as a murder victim. Back home, the homicide cop I've worked with says confessions always seem to pop up with any high-profile murder. They keep certain information secret to weed out the fake ones."

"Exactly. It's possible there are two killers."

Oh my. If Eddie had been attacked and hit over the head, then Dixie came home and found him, what a symbolic gesture to grab a knife and stab the heartbreaker. To break his heart in retaliation for his treatment of her.

My thoughts were swirling so rapidly that I missed the next thing Pen said.

"I was simply wondering aloud what our next steps should be. I'm afraid all of our crime solving has centered around thefts and con artists, no murders."

"So far."

"Yes, right. So far." Pen sighed loudly enough that I heard the frustration.

Chapter 20

My first thought was to check back with Detective Hernandez and to find out what had happened with Sophie. As long as my young charge was safe, was it really my job to find out whether her mother had murdered the boyfriend? I wanted to think not. I *wanted* to go home.

I pulled out the business card he'd given me and dialed.

"Ah, yes, the lady from Albuquerque," he said when I introduced myself.

I could hear papers shuffling in the background and pictured him at a desk laden with the folders of a dozen unsolved cases. At least that's what Kent Taylor's desk normally looks like. I asked about Sophie, whether they'd found a safe place for her.

"We have. In fact, the department social worker was just here ten minutes ago. She's done the necessary paperwork to place Sophie in temporary custody with a Grace Nelson and family." More paper shuffling, a mild curse as something dropped with a clunk. "I'm told Sophie spent the night in a holding cell here, alone, not in the general population. Today, Mrs. Nelson will be coming down to finalize the forms and take her home. It will be a monitored situation, with our department checking regularly."

Maybe the Mesa police were less understaffed than many other departments. I couldn't imagine them having the time to follow up with a teen in foster care when there were crimes to be solved. Speaking of which … "Is there any news about locating the killer of Edward Peppard?"

"Dixie O'Connell is our lead suspect."

"Surely no—"

"The murder took place in her home where the victim was living with her in a domestic relationship, there was little sign of a struggle, and the knife was one from her own kitchen set. The scenario is more common than you'd like to think."

That was probably true.

"But so many pieces don't fit," I said. "Dixie knew Sophie would be returning home, was planning on it. She told her daughter Eddie would be home in case she couldn't get there herself quite on time."

"And if this homecoming was such an anticipated event, why wouldn't the mother make every effort to be there herself?"

I couldn't exactly answer that.

"We're making inquiries along all lines, ma'am. We will apprehend the killer, and we'll build an airtight case that she won't be able to deny. By the way, you are free to leave the city now."

He gave a curt good-day and hung up.

I flopped onto one of the stools at the counter. *She can't deny?* Wow. Talk about presumptions. The man had made up his mind already. I phoned Pen.

"Oh, heavens. That doesn't sound good, Charlie."

"No, it doesn't. He said I could leave, but … I just can't help putting myself in Sophie's fancy red boots and thinking of how this would go for her."

"Absolutely. Unless her mother is cleared, she'll end up spending the next five years or more in the foster care system."

"I need to talk with the girl before I make any decision to go back to Albuquerque."

"Yes, excellent thinking. I've got a board meeting this morning for the Ames Foundation, but I shall be eager to hear what more you learn about this whole situation."

I thanked Pen again for providing the autopsy information this morning, then I called Gracie.

"Charlie! Glad you called. I've got Sophie with me. Just picked her up from downtown and we're on our way to my house. She's in desperate need of a shower and some comfort food. I promised spaghetti for lunch. Want to join us?"

Sophie's voice in the background was saying, "Yes, Charlie, come!"

I got the address and said I'd love some lunch.

Gracie met me at the covered porch of her Tempe home, a nice mid-size place in another of those cookie-cutter neighborhoods ubiquitous throughout the valley. The Nelson home had pale gray stucco with charcoal gray trim, mature trees in the front yard, and pots of brilliant marigolds on the front steps.

"How's Sophie doing?" I asked in a low voice. I assumed the reason Gracie had stepped outside to greet me was so that we could speak privately for a minute.

"Pretty good, considering. I didn't get much out of her about her time in New Mexico when she ran away from home. Mostly she seems concerned about her mom."

"Understandably. Well, we'll see what we can learn that might help us find Dixie." I gave the one-sentence synopsis of what Hernandez had said and his attitude.

I heard a sound behind me and turned to see Sophie had opened the front door. She wore stretch jeans and a cute red top with the red boots. Her blonde hair hung down her back in damp strands. She actually smiled at me. Most remarkably, I didn't see her cell phone in her hands. I turned toward her and received a hug. What a switch from two days ago!

"Feeling better?"

"Yeah, the shower helped. That place last night smelled like some creepy disinfectant."

"The kind that makes you wonder if the place is bug infested?"

"Yeah. Uck." She caught me looking at her boots. "Like 'em? My mom and I got matching ones."

"Ah." That answered my question about whether Dixie and her daughter shared clothes.

We walked inside, where the aroma of tomatoey sauce filled the air. "Spaghetti Bolognese is my specialty," Gracie said, hurrying through the foyer and great room to the kitchen and giving a quick stir to the pot of sauce. A large kettle was steaming on another burner. She picked up a handful of long spaghetti and fed it into the boiling water.

"We rented the house out while we were in Thailand

for several months. I'm glad we didn't sell, but I'm still having to search for things that got put away in different places. Case in point, my grater for the parmesan."

She had a special grater just for that? My culinary skills are so unrefined, I'm doing well to remember to set out the jar the cheese comes in from the store. Gracie had set the dining table with three places; a large bowl of salad sat there, something she had probably whipped together with her eyes closed.

As the pasta pot bubbled, I took a seat at the counter. Sophie had disappeared, but just as I was about to bring up the case with Gracie, the teen came back. Her hair was dry now and the phone was back in her hand. She set it on the counter and sat next to me.

"I'm glad you stayed," she said. "Gracie says you're going to help figure out where my mom is. The cops won't tell me anything. Plus, I have more faith in you and the Heist Ladies than them."

I nodded. "I hope we can find your mom and get this whole thing straightened out. Have you heard from her? I mean, since yesterday when …"

She gave a wistful look toward the phone and shook her head.

"Lunch is ready," Gracie announced. "Come in and dish up your plates."

We helped ourselves to the perfectly cooked pasta and sauce, then took seats at the table. Sophie dug in as if she hadn't eaten in a week, while I marveled at the effort for what was *just* lunch. At home a meal this size would have been a major dinner production.

Sophie cleaned her plate and took a small second portion. We kept conversation on the lighter side, for her sake. Although I was dying to dig into the case and find some answers, I didn't want to send her off the deep end by letting on that her mother was the target of Hernandez's investigation.

She set down her fork and picked up her phone, automatically scrolling through her texts, apparently finding nothing new. When she set it aside and announced she was feeling really sleepy, I held out my hand for the phone.

"Do you mind if I look through the messages from your mom? Maybe I'll spot something in what she says, some little clue."

I was a little bit amazed when she handed over the precious device and nodded before wandering away down the hall toward the bedrooms. Gracie and I exchanged a look.

Chapter 21

Gracie had to smile as she cleared the table and put away the leftovers. Charlie had accessed Sophie's phone the moment the girl closed her bedroom door. She sat now at the kitchen counter, reading through messages.

"We *have* to find Dixie. If Hernandez gets hold of her first, it's probably all over. He'll quit looking at anyone else."

"At least we might find some other viable suspects. We know this Eddie had a reputation with other women as well." Gracie stopped short of naming Linda. Given their friend's delicate health, she surely couldn't have actually wielded the knife. Could she?

Or could Linda, knowing she was dying anyway, use that as the perfect justification for doing away with the man who'd caused her—and her daughter—so much anguish?

"Rosalie," Gracie said aloud. "She did say something the other day …"

Charlie looked up from the phone screen. "Hmm, I hadn't thought about that. Worth checking her out. Maybe we can figure out whether she and Linda have alibis."

"Unless we know the time of Eddie's death, it's going to be tough to pin that down, isn't it? Just saying he died on Wednesday, or whenever, is not very precise."

"True. We could check back with Pen and see if she can learn more from her inside sources." Charlie looked up and stared out the kitchen window for a long moment. "You know … I had been thinking the man who pounded on my motel room door in the early hours on Friday might have been Eddie. Maybe somehow he knew Sophie was in the room and had come after her … but that can't be. By Friday morning he was already dead."

"Which means Pen's and my trip to Holbrook—the tip we'd received—that was based on outdated info as well."

They thought about that for a moment before Charlie went back to the phone screen. "There are a lot of texts back and forth between Dixie and her daughter on Thursday. That's the day I picked Sophie up in Santa Fe. Some on Friday and just one on Saturday, which is when I began to suspect someone else had gotten hold of Dixie's phone and was faking messages."

"Either that or Dixie was establishing an alibi earlier, then knew she didn't need to after Friday?" Gracie held up both hands. "Just saying. At this point we have no way of knowing. Is there anything in the messages that would indicate where she was when she sent them?"

Charlie shook her head. "I can't tell anything by them." She paused and sat up a little straighter. "Do you suppose Amber could figure it out? Would there be a way for us to send her the information?"

"My guess is that she would need the actual phone, or access to the account so she could … I don't know … look at the cloud or something. I really have no clue how all that works."

"It's early enough in the evening to reach her, isn't it? Can we try a call?"

"Sure." Gracie picked up her phone and tapped a number, waiting for the international connection to go through.

Charlie snapped screenshots of the texts and forwarded them to her own phone, in case they would be of help.

Amber came on and they switched to video chat so she could see the phone the women were asking about. "Is it password protected?" was her first question.

"I don't think so. Sophie handed it over to me and it came right back to life when I touched the screen."

"Okay, that's good. I can walk you through some steps where we can look at the texting history."

"What we're after is the location of someone else who was texting to this phone," Charlie explained.

Amber's expression faded. "Not so sure about that. Give me the phone's data and I'll see if maybe I can figure out a way to clone it." She talked Charlie through a series of steps, took the information, but didn't give a lot of hope.

"What would be most useful is to know the location of Dixie at the time of the last message she sent to her daughter. We're trying to find her so we can ask questions."

"Did you try calling her? You've got her daughter's phone in hand. If she sees Sophie's name, she'll probably answer."

Gracie and Charlie looked at each other, incredulous.

"Guess that's why you get the big bucks," Gracie said with a laugh.

Charlie seemed a little doubtful. After all, Sophie had said she'd tried calling her mom numerous times during these past two days. But she went into the contacts and gave Dixie's number a tap. Over the speaker, it rang and rang, finally connecting to a voicemail message.

"Hey, it's Dixie! If there's a party, definitely leave me a message. If it's something boring, well okay, you can leave a message too and I'll call you back after the party!"

Charlie spoke: "Sorry this is one of the boring ones, but we really need to talk to you. The police are looking for you. Sophie is staying with a friend and she's really worried." She left her name and cell number, in hopes that Dixie might do both—reassure her daughter and call Charlie before the police found her.

"Okay, so much for that," Amber said. "I'll see what I can dig up. Talk later."

Gracie turned to Charlie, who was adding Sophie's and Dixie's numbers to her own phone. "What about other texts Sophie might have received in recent days? Is Eddie one of her contacts?"

"Good idea to take a peek." Charlie glanced down the hall, where Sophie's bedroom door was still closed.

She went into the list of texts and scrolled through. "Ah-ha—Eddie's name *is* here. She has him in her list as Dee."

"Huh?"

"Her mother's nickname for him."

Charlie went into the recent calls, finding nothing to or from Eddie. In the texting history, she did spot his name. All the messages were older, the newest dating back more than a month. "Interesting that Eddie was texting Sophie while she was technically a runaway."

"Yeah, that's kind of weird. What do they say?"

"The most recent? Mind your own business, you little bitch." Charlie thumbed the screen upward. "I'm thinking we better go back to the beginning of this whole conversation."

Chapter 22

I found myself fascinated as I went down the rabbit hole of Sophie's text conversations. The journey went like this:

July 15, 9:21 a.m.– You're my ride to soccer practice. Mom says.

July 15, 9:22 a.m. – Yep, see you in ten.

July 21, 1:45 p.m. – Need that ride home … where ru? (smiley emoji)

July 21, 2:17 p.m. – Had some biz, there in a minute

August 4, 5:19 p.m. – Mom says grab chicken on your way home

August 4, 5:23 p.m. – Right.

"That all sounds pretty much like any family," Gracie said. She was filling the tea kettle at the kitchen sink.

August 15, 2:31 p.m. – Dee! Waiting on you here. What up? (angry face emoji)

August 15, 2:47 p.m. – Hold on. Biz holdup. Give me half hour.

August 15, 2:48 p.m. – Business? What, at the casino?

August 15, 2:49 p.m. – Business, as in none of yours. I'll be there when I get there.

August 15, 2:50 p.m. – Fine, I'll call mom instead.

August 15, 2:51 p.m. – I'm in the car now, ten min away.

"The battle shapes up," I said as Gracie set a cup of tea on the counter in front of me. "Eddie's probably out doing things he shouldn't and Sophie's basically blackmailing him into compliance."

Gracie chuckled. "Yeah, every kid uses the 'I'll tell Mom' or 'I'll tell Dad' line to get their own way. Still, it does sound like Dixie was counting on Eddie to be Sophie's ride during the summer months, and he wasn't very reliable."

"Here we go into September. School must have started by this time."

Sept 9, 12:23 p.m. – (finger-shaking emoji) Naughty boy Saw you at the brew pub at lunch

Sept 9, 12:49 p.m. – Business, that's all. You need a ride after school?

Sept 9, 12:51 p.m. – Duh, got the bus

Sept 10, 3:40 p.m. – Check your room when you get home. Got you a present.

"Hm, no response to that one. The next is about a week later."

Sept 16, 8: 47 p.m. – You bribing me? Three presents in four days? Mom knows. This won't work.

Sept 16, 11:19 p.m. – Knows what?

Sept 16, 11:50 p.m. – oh come on! The women. The gray haired one and the cute young blonde. Mom's no dummy.

"Ooh—things are heating up." Gracie leaned across

the counter and took a peek at the phone screen. "I'm surprised she wasn't intimidated about accusing him directly like that."

"Well, *something* happened. The very next, and last, message is the one I read first, where he tells her to mind her own business. Then, silence."

"What about messages between Sophie and her mom?"

"Let's just check that out …" I glanced again toward the bedrooms. No change.

I went back to the messages screen and found the thread with Dixie. The most recent were Sophie's outgoing texts asking where her mom was, sent over the past few days. Contrary to what the girl had told me, there were no responses. Her mom was not telling her that Eddie would be there to meet her; she gave no clues as to her own whereabouts.

Gracie's forehead wrinkled when I told her all of it. "This isn't good. What if something has happened to Dixie?"

Lots of possibilities. The woman could be hiding out from the boyfriend, or she could be hiding from the authorities.

I scrolled upward, to see the older messages. Back in July and August, everything followed along with the communications between Eddie and Sophie. He was giving the girl rides to various places she needed to be. Dixie referred to being tied up at work. I needed to learn more about that. I'd been under the impression Dixie didn't have a job. But she obviously had some commitment if she needed her boyfriend to act as shuttle service for her kid.

By late August and early September, things were getting tense:

Sept 2, 4:05 p.m. – Sorry baby. Dee got tied up. I'll send you an Uber.

Sept 9, 11:15 a.m. – Saw Dee when me and friends left campus for lunch

Sept 9, 11:16 a.m. – Eddie near your school? Don't think so. He had a meeting downtown.

Sept 9, 12:17 p.m. – Mom. Seriously? Wake up. He wasn't alone.

Sept 9, 2:01 p.m. – Don't worry, I'll take care of him. You need a ride today?

Sept 9, 2:02 p.m. – Nope. Don't want to ride with him anyway.

Sept 9, 2:04 p.m. – Let's have a nice family dinner tonight, talk things out.

Sept 9, 2:05 p.m. – Whatever. Repeat—wake up!

Things continued in that vein for another week, then:

Sept 20, 6:40 p.m. – Sophie, where you? Dinner's on.

Sept 20, 6:41 p.m. – Not coming. Look in my room.

Sept 20, 6:45 p.m. – What the hell, baby? Leaving? Where are you, who are you with?

Sept 20, 6:47 p.m. – The note explains. Can't live there with Dee. NO MORE!

Elena Garcia had told me Sophie was on the road for a couple months. This explained when it happened and how she informed her mother.

Gracie spoke up. "Yeah, I'm not surprised. As we were driving home from downtown this morning, Sophie told me about a couple of massive fights between her mom and Eddie. And yet, Dixie didn't immediately dump this creep and let her daughter know it was safe to come home? Wow." She seemed stunned at the idea a woman would choose a man over her own kid.

"It happens. I cannot explain why."

She sighed. "She's young and irresponsible, and that's probably exactly why."

Another thought occurred to me. "Maybe Dixie knew all about Eddie's behavior but by this time he'd cleaned her out financially? She was either dependent on him, or she hoped to figure out a way to get her money back."

I scanned quickly through the rest of the texts, switched the phone over to its home screen, and placed it in a casual position at the other end of the counter hoping Sophie wouldn't realize the depth of my intrusion into her personal life.

Gracie must have read my mind. "Wouldn't the police have seen all this during the time she was in their custody?"

I thought about that. "Can't say for sure, but my guess would be that since Sophie wasn't a suspect in their case, they had no grounds to demand her phone, not without a court order. Now—if Dixie does get arrested for the murder and they're building a case against her, yeah, then they'll reach for every communication that could prove to be evidence."

"I wish we had Dixie's phone. Messages and calls between her and Eddie could prove enlightening." Gracie was still on the move in her kitchen, pulling some food items from the upper cupboards.

"No kidding. Dixie's phone … it's a puzzle to me. Since we have no idea where the woman actually is right now, I keep asking myself if she even has her phone with her. What if it's fallen into someone else's hands and that person sent the most recent texts to Sophie?"

"I suppose that's possible. Any way to verify it?"

Again, my doubts as to whether I had actually spoken

to Dixie. I thought of one possibility, and pulled my phone from my pocket.

Elena Garcia answered right away, which was nice. In my eagerness to wrap things up and get home, even the delay of leaving messages and waiting for callbacks was grating.

"Elena! You're in your office."

"Oh, yes. The government wheels only slow down on official holidays."

"Can you look in your notes and tell me when was the last time you actually spoke personally with Dixie O'Connell, Sophie's mother?"

"Um, sure. Let me switch mental gears here real quick."

"Thanks. Sorry for interrupting but it's really important."

"Has something happened?"

"Many somethings. But Sophie is safe and it's all going to get sorted out." I could be on the phone for hours if I went into the whole story.

"Okay, good." She was bursting with curiosity, I could tell. "Let's take a look at my phone log here … Dixie O'Connell's number is in the log the morning that you picked up Sophie."

"Did you actually speak with her? Hear her voice?"

"I assume so. I mean, yes, I did speak with a woman. She answered at the number provided to me by the daughter, and she identified herself. Sophie seemed satisfied. Charlie, what's going on?"

I gave only the bare-bones version. I'd arrived in Mesa to find that Dixie was not home and we'd not been able to reach her. Sophie was in the care of a reliable friend until the authorities could find her mother. I thanked Elena for her information and hung up.

"Well. Are we any further along?" Gracie stopped in mid stride and looked up.

Sophie was standing there, no longer sleepy at all. "What's going on?"

Chapter 23

R eady to bake some pies?" Gracie said in a perky voice. I was antsy to be doing something toward heading home. Whatever that might be, it wasn't going to happen while hanging around Gracie's house all day. Besides, maybe Gracie could get more information from Sophie without me around.

"Sophie, you said something about doing some laundry? If you'll gather up your clothes, we'll put a load in the washer while I teach you my own special recipe for pumpkin pie."

I had to admire Gracie's natural feel for being a mom. Get the kid busy doing a task so you could talk about them. I needed to remember that.

"I'm going to try something else to locate Dixie," I said in a low tone. "If Sophie tells you anything of importance or if she should happen to hear from her mom, let me know right away."

"Will do."

I was digging out my car keys when Sophie walked in with an armload of clothes. It couldn't hurt to ask her for ideas. Otherwise, I was down to visiting the police station to see if Hernandez would share.

"Sophie, got a second?"

A nod.

"I thought I'd try some other ways to find your mom. Maybe some of her social friends or her coworkers would know where she went?"

She shrugged in that noncommittal way of hers. "I called her best friend Jenna, you know, to see if they'd been out partying. She said no."

"Could you give me Jenna's number? Maybe she's thought of something since you talked to her."

She dropped the clothes on the floor and reached to the countertop for her phone. I input the number into mine.

"Thanks. I'll see you later."

When I walked out of the house, Sophie was getting a lesson on the laundry settings for Gracie's washer, and there were already pie ingredients all around the kitchen. Those two would do just fine without me around. I glanced at the clock as I left Gracie's neighborhood.

Still most of the afternoon and all evening to do some sleuthing, although I should check in with Sandy at some point. I so seldom stay in someone else's home that I'm not really up on the protocols. No doubt it would be considered rude to vanish until bedtime. Sandy seemed like the type who would fuss, want to make dinner plans and all that. Maybe I should have insisted on being in a hotel. Oh well, a little late to make that choice now.

Since I had no clue where I would go next, I pulled into a Home Depot parking lot and phoned Dixie's friend Jenna. She sounded breathless when she answered.

"Sorry … I'm on the treadmill … Who'd you say this is?"

I explained while she huffed and puffed. A couple of electronic beeps sounded in the background and the machine came to a halt.

"Okay, I can hear you better now. Did you say Dixie is missing?"

"We think so. She hasn't been home and her daughter can't reach her by phone."

"Ohhh, that's not good." The background noise level changed as she walked into another room. "I've been a little worried myself."

"When was the last time you talked to her?"

"Talked? Maybe a week. Texted a time or two after that, then complete silence. She hasn't returned either calls or texts from me in a while."

"She was supposed to be home Thursday evening to meet me and Sophie. We got delayed, but haven't got hold of her yet. She told Sophie that Eddie would be there to meet us Friday. Is that typical for her, to have Eddie look after her daughter?"

There was a sputter. "Over the summer, yeah, probably. But in recent months, no way."

Which kind of confirmed what I'd suspected. Either Sophie made that up so I'd leave her alone at the house, or someone other than Dixie had used her phone. I followed that thread with Jenna. "Problems?"

"Oh yeah. The bloom was off the romance, and Dixie

was having a hard time getting rid of the guy. You ever wanted to break up a relationship, ask the person to leave, and they simply wouldn't go? I told her to change the locks and toss all his shit out in the driveway. There's more than one way to get rid of a bum."

"It appears she never did that. He still had a key."

"I was afraid of that. You know that he was pressuring her to put him on the title to her house? Can you believe it?"

After hearing Linda's story, I actually could. But I didn't say so.

"I had the impression Eddie had lots of money of his own …"

"He's a charmer, all right. Spends a lot, shows a woman a good time. But it's all on credit. He got himself added to Dixie's main credit card shortly after they met, and he ran that thing up, *way* up. Mostly buying stuff for her that she didn't even want. She kept a pretty close eye on the statements, suspected he was spending at the casinos. But she said that never showed up."

"Maybe he was making cash withdrawals and using that to gamble."

"I don't know. I think she would have said something. He's cagey though. He could figure out something."

I noticed Jenna was talking about Eddie in the present tense. She must not have heard the news stories. I wasn't sure whether to inform her, but it seemed rotten not to. When I told her he was dead, she actually gasped.

"Oh. My. God. Oh, Dixie, what have you done …?"

"Jenna …? Do you actually think Dixie had something to do with this?"

"No. No! I really don't, and I didn't mean to give that

impression. Forget I said anything. Please don't pass that comment along to anyone, okay?"

"I won't." At least not to the police. No doubt I *would* share it with the Heist Ladies. "One other thing, Jenna, and I'll let you go. Can you tell me where Dixie works? Sophie was really vague. I'm hoping maybe a coworker has heard from her."

"Love of Dogs. That's what it's called. They find homes for rescue dogs. Dixie loves the work, even though it doesn't pay anything really." She gave me an address and basic directions to a place not far from Dixie's house.

I thanked her profusely for the additional insights.

"Tell her to call me," Jenna said. "I can't stand it that there's all this trouble happening in her life and I haven't even known about it."

"I will."

I sat in the parking lot another few minutes, looking up directions to this rescue place and scrolling through the pictures on their website. I'm such a sucker for dogs, especially those with a sad story attached. Each of my own dogs in recent years were abandoned and just took up with me. I braced myself for the challenge of walking into this place and walking out without a carload of additional pets.

Chapter 24

The noise level was a little insane, most likely because a newcomer had entered the facility and every dog in there was calling out, "Pick me, pick me!" in its own woofy way. I started with the simplest tactic when I approached the middle-aged woman at the front desk.

"I'm trying to make contact with an old friend and I heard she works here. Dixie O'Connell. Is she here today?" Once in a while this actually works. We've had cases where the person left home and family behind but still reported for the job.

The woman smiled up at me with somewhat tea-stained teeth. "I'm afraid not. Can someone else help you?"

I didn't bother to point out that if Dixie was my friend, it was unlikely someone else could immediately fill that position. I just smiled back.

"Sorry," she said, realizing how her answer sounded. "Maybe you'd want to talk with Carleen. She and Dixie are also acquainted outside work and she'd know more than I do."

She led me through a door to a room lined by chain link enclosures. Most were empty, and I wondered where all the barking had come from. We walked down the little corridor in the center of the room, out a back door, and into a yard area that must be nearly an acre in size. Dogs immediately rushed us.

"Oh my goodness, look at you," I said to the little black and white mutt who jumped up with front paws on my knee, its little face eager to befriend me. It looked like a border collie crossed with a terrier of some kind. Four others crowded around and I couldn't help but laugh at their sweet expressions.

"Carleen? You out here?" shouted the woman who'd brought me out.

"Right here!" A younger woman—early thirties, I'd guess—with short, perky blonde hair emerged from a small shed. She wore denim capris and a fitted t-shirt, had very tan arms and legs, and carried a bucket of dry kibble in each hand. The moment the dogs saw her, she became their new favorite person.

The receptionist lady walked away so I approached Carleen and introduced myself, not bothering with the friend-of-Dixie ruse. She set the food buckets on a picnic table and reached out to shake my hand.

"I can see why this place is named Love of Dogs. Wow, I'm impressed with how many there are and how well everyone gets along."

"Most do great together. Dogs are pack creatures and

they normally thrive in families. We actually have probably twice this many, but a lot are fostered out to homes, people who'll take in three or four and help socialize them for adoption. A few are strays or abandoned pets from the area, but the majority come to us from Mexico. The stray dog population there is huge—people don't neuter their animals and many are left to roam the streets and breed like crazy. There's a fantastic rescue place near one of the small towns there where a lady and her crew of volunteers take them in—sick, injured, pregnant, whole litters of puppies. She works with the local vets to get them healthy, spayed and neutered. When she gets upwards of two hundred dogs at once, she'll bring vanloads of them up to Arizona where several shelters, like us, take over and find forever homes for them."

"What a great cause." My heart went out to the eager little faces all around. Now that Carleen had told me about their origins, I could see that these guys definitely came from the same mix of the gene pool. I had to resist getting down on the ground and hugging all of them.

"I actually came here in hopes of talking with Dixie O'Connell. I understand she works here?"

"Yeah. I got her started here after her husband passed away. It was pretty sudden and she seemed kind of lost. She and I … well, we always liked to go out for drinks, dance a little, have some fun. We met at the gym a few years back and decided partying was a lot more fun than lifting weights." Her laugh was infectious.

"So, now … The lady up front said Dixie hasn't been in?" I gave the basics of how Sophie had come into my realm and we needed to get mother and daughter back together.

A wrinkle crossed Carleen's forehead. "No, and I haven't heard from her either. Well, I take that back. A week or so ago she asked the boss for some personal time. Something's been going on between her and Eddie. I don't know what. I loved them as a couple—so fun and cute together. But then something changed. She got really down on him. He told me—" A funny little smile crossed her face.

I waited a very long moment.

"Oh, never mind. It's their business." She picked up the food buckets.

"Um, well. It *was* their business. Eddie's dead."

Her face went sort of ashy under the tan. She obviously hadn't known. She squeezed her eyes shut and took a deep breath. When she opened them, she didn't look directly at me.

Did I detect something between Eddie and Carleen? It was subtle but there was something … as if she was taking his side. She seemed devastated, but was trying not to show it to me. Had the three of them …? I shook off the feeling. I was after facts here. I could process all the information later.

I trailed along as she started walking toward a monster-sized tray that apparently served as the feeding bowl for a dozen dogs at once. She scattered kibble in it and moved to a second one. Clearly she was busy and distracted, and had said all she intended. I thanked her for the information and handed her one of my cards.

"Please, if you hear anything at all from Dixie, let me know. Or have her get in touch with me. Sophie is alone now and pretty scared. We really need to find her mom."

I headed back toward the door I'd come out through,

the one that led through the kennel area, reception, and back to the parking lot. A young man was lining a wheeled garbage can with a trash bag. Judging by the pooper-scooper tools beside it, I guessed what his job was.

"Is Dixie going to be okay?" he asked, as I started to walk past.

"Excuse me?"

"I overheard you asking Carleen about her, about where Dixie is now."

"Yeah, I'm getting really concerned."

He nodded. "I am too. There was some kind of serious shit going down last week, and then she just ghosted us. No one knows what happened."

"Do you think she's been harmed?"

He picked up the small rake and shovel and gave a big shrug. "Don't know. Wouldn't be surprised."

I slipped him a card, too, and left with the same request that he contact me if he learned anything more.

Behind the wheel of the Highlander again, I pondered what I'd heard. What if Eddie had harmed Dixie? My head began to buzz—if he'd somehow gained access to her finances, they'd fought, and he could get away with killing her, would he? But then who killed him? I'd pegged Dixie as a prime suspect, and she still might qualify. But the fact that her coworkers had doubts about her safety … well, that put a whole new twist on things. Who could benefit by both of them being dead?

Sophie.

Chapter 25

Sophie was the only person who claimed to have spoken with Dixie in the past week, if I didn't count Elena Garcia, and she probably wouldn't absolutely know the mother's voice. Sophie could have faked the phone calls and maybe the texts too if she had possession of her mother's phone. But how?

She'd been on the run for more than two months, and we knew Dixie had been at work up until a week ago. Sophie was in some kind of official custody during that week. All of it? Maybe.

My head was starting to pound again.

There was one way I could at least prove or disprove one aspect of the argument. I went back inside the dog place, walked through to the back and found Carleen.

"Did Dixie say anything, say, in the past two or three

months, about losing her cell phone? Having to get a new one?"

The blonde stared into space for a long time. "No. If she did, she didn't say anything to me. I still have the same number for her."

"Okay, thanks. It was just a thought."

"No problem." She dumped the last of the food from the second bucket into the remaining feeder tray. Every dog in the place was munching down, quickly, when I left.

My mind still wouldn't settle, but at least I had more data to process than I'd arrived with. Maybe Amber could offer ideas on the questions about Dixie's phone. I pulled out of the parking area into massively heavy traffic. I hate the rush hour in Albuquerque but it's nothing compared to this. It would take a while to get to Sandy's house, and I remembered we hadn't exactly made plans for the evening. Still, I didn't want to take my attention off the road even long enough to activate a hands-free call.

I glanced at the sign for the next cross street and saw it was Brown Road. Figuring I could accomplish two things, I made the turn. Dixie's address came up sooner than I expected, something like a half-block later, so I quickly whipped into her small development.

Finding her house was simple enough—it still had the crime scene tape around the yard. The house was dark and there were no official vehicles in sight. I rolled to a stop in front of the property. I was *so* tempted to see if I could find a way in—I did know the secret to opening Sophie's bedroom window, after all.

What could I discover in there? Blood on the kitchen floor, a knife missing from the block on the counter. I already knew about those. However, a prowl through Dixie's bedroom could reveal all kinds of excellent secrets.

Anything from a fight scene with Eddie, a restraining order to make him leave, to her cell phone. That little piece of technology alone could answer a bunch of my questions.

But that would be dumb. One: the crime scene folks might not be done, and they'd return to find my prints in a flash; Two: I could get caught in the act; Three: They'd been through the place already and had no doubt taken all the good stuff away with them.

I took my eyes off the house and called Sandy.

"Charlie! I was just about to call you. Mind reader."

I told her where I was and asked if I should pick up food and come to her house.

"Don't worry about that. Pen suggested we all get together. We have a favorite sushi place here in Mesa. She and Mary are already holding a table for us. Where are you?"

"Sitting at the curb in front of Dixie O'Connell's house."

"Oooh—is she there?"

"Nope, the place looks dark and empty."

"So, you're only five or ten minutes from the sushi place. If that sounds good to you, just drive on over. Of course, if you'd rather have an evening alone I understand that, and you're welcome to come back to my place. Heckle and Jeckle won't talk your ear off too much."

Tempting as it sounded to have a space all to myself, I was here to get answers so I could head home soon. "Will Sophie be there?"

"Um, no. Gracie has her whole family at home tonight, so they're staying in."

Which was perfectly fine with me. I'd need the chance to talk about the teen and her mom, and that would have been awkward. I told Sandy I'd love to join the group for dinner.

"See you in a few," she said after giving me directions.

I'd just located a parking spot when I saw Sandy drive up. It turned out the restaurant was fairly central between Dixie's place and Sandy's.

"If you like sushi, you'll love this place," Sandy said as we walked up to the door of the small sushi bar and teppanyaki restaurant. My nod assured her I loved it. "Order the Las Vegas roll. It's amazing. Of course, we usually get a whole assortment of rolls and everyone shares."

"The only way to do it," I said with a smile.

The booths had nice, high divider walls so conversation could stay private—the perfect layout. Sandy and I slid in across from Pen and Mary.

"How was your day?" Mary asked, once we'd clinked our wine glasses and placed the food order.

I filled them in on everything, from Gracie's and my snooping Sophie's cell phone this afternoon to my visit to the dog rescue.

"No one has seen or heard from Dixie in a week. I tell you, it was really tempting to sneak into that empty house to see if I could find her phone or some clue as to where she is right now."

"The police will surely be finished there by tomorrow," Mary said. "We could—"

Sandy put her fingers in her ears. "Lalalala … I cannot be hearing this kind of talk."

Pen laughed.

"After plotting out exactly how I'd get in, I realized if there was anything of value to be learned, the police would have already bagged and tagged it. I'd go to all that trouble and end up SOL."

"Okay, probably true," Mary admitted. "But a call to Detective Hernandez probably couldn't hurt. You know, the excuse being that Sophie is in Gracie's care and we wonder if they found anything on her mother's whereabouts."

"He wouldn't tell us anything specific," I said, "but even a yes or no answer could be helpful."

Nods all around.

"I want to follow through on Sophie's accusations to Eddie about his gambling habits. That's a way to rack up a *lot* of debt in a short time. If we found out where he gambled and got an idea of how much, it would certainly make the case for why he was after both Linda's and Dixie's money."

"Not to mention offering up some hard-cash motives for murder," Pen said. "Just thinking aloud, because this could make a great plot for my next book."

"And once we find some other people with motives, we can try to pin down each of them on their whereabouts when Eddie was killed." Mary took another sip of her wine.

"Except that we don't know what time that was. We've only been given a ballpark idea within a range that includes all of last weekend."

"True. A bit too vague to be helpful." Pen looked up and spotted our waiter, who had both hands full.

We received five platters loaded with such an array of flavors. I have to admit, I lost myself in savoring them with plenty of ginger and wasabi. Sandy was right about the Las Vegas roll. The crispy battered edges were sheer perfection. Conversation dwindled, and within twenty minutes there were only some smudges of sauce on the serving plates.

That's when Pen's phone chimed. The waiter, who had

been about to offer more wine or some dessert, backed away.

Pen's expression changed from a relaxed smile to one of consternation. "Oh, no. God. What hospital?"

Everyone's attention riveted on her as she thanked the caller and ended the call.

"It's Linda."

Chapter 26

The hospital was in Scottsdale, apparently the closest one to Linda's home. We piled into one vehicle and Sandy got us there in record time. Pen, especially, was quiet. No doubt thinking of her long friendship with Linda.

"I watched Rosalie grow up, almost as a niece to me. She sounded stricken, just now on the phone."

I reached across the back seat and placed a hand on her shoulder. She patted my hand and gave me a brave smile. Sandy found parking and we all trooped inside, locating the elevators and making our way to the room where Rosalie had told Pen she'd be waiting.

Four of us arriving at once seemed a bit much for the hospital staff, a couple of whom gave us the stink eye. Rosalie went straight to Pen and gave her a long hug, then the two of them went into the room. Through a window I could see the tiny shape of Linda in the bed, with an array of tubes and wires leading to beeping machines behind her. After a few minutes, Rosalie came out and suggested some others could take her place and visit.

I was the logical one to stay outside. Linda didn't really know me; we'd met only once.

"She's dying," Rosalie said simply. "It's been a long battle with the cancer, and she fought it bravely, but she's ready. She told me that last week. She said the next hospital trip would be her last."

I didn't know what to say. I could only imagine how exhausting it must be to endure years of medical appointments, repeated tests, treatments that felt worse than the disease itself. I turned to the daughter who seemed equally fatigued.

"How are you holding up?"

"I alternate between the grief that's always right here, near the edges, and this sort of angry furor over what Edward Peppard did to her."

"The things you were telling us the other day?"

"That, and more. Since I've begun to realize these are Mother's final days, I've gotten all her papers from the safe deposit box and begun going through them. It's shocking how much he talked her out of. And not just money—travel, expensive clothes, a sports car, two antique cars, cosmetic surgery! Yes, he had a facelift that she paid for."

We had drifted toward a small alcove waiting area where we could be alone, and she glanced around, keeping her voice down as we took a couple of the chairs.

"And *then*—then he somehow talked her into changing her trust documents to include him in the inheritance. I think I mentioned before that he's claiming rights to her home. Publicly, he made it seem like they were married.

Eddie wanted it to seem like he was this doting husband because he always took her arm, opened doors for her, ran little errands, brought home her favorite foods ... Thank goodness she never married him or he might actually have some community property rights to everything. I asked her about that, and I verified it through public records. As I said, around others they both went along with the pretense. Mother's from that generation where living together was considered a sin and she was happy enough to let people believe Edward had made an 'honest woman' of her."

"But the inheritance?"

"Oh, she did that, all right. I don't know what she was thinking. I'm absolutely certain he talked her into it, just as he talked her out of hundreds of thousands of dollars for various schemes of his. He'd propose something as a *business* deal, but I know he was losing it at the casinos." She pressed her fingertips to her temples. "It was going to cost me a hefty amount to pay him off and make him go away."

And now that Eddie was dead, Rosalie was off the hook for all of that.

She read my expression. "Oh no ... you don't think ... Sure, I *wanted* to kill him... but I didn't, and neither did Mother. They need to look at someone else." The implication being, look at Dixie.

I had my doubts as to whether Linda was physically strong enough to have performed the deed. Rosalie, yes. She was young enough, strong enough, and full of fire on this subject.

"Just be careful how much of this story you relate to others. The police are investigating Eddie's death and they're going to see everything you just told me as a pretty strong motive."

"I don't even know when he actually died."

"It's a bit vague, since he wasn't found right away. I think the medical examiner narrowed it down to sometime last Thursday night or Friday morning." I edged a glance toward her. "Do you and your mother have alibis for that timeframe? In case the police come around and ask?"

"I'm sure we were at home. Our routine had settled into one of having light meals, my dispensing Mother's medications, an early bedtime. Normally it was just the two of us. I'll go back through my calendar and see if anything else shows up. Really, the days and nights have been a blur in recent weeks."

"I understand."

A nurse peeked around the corner. "Oh, there you are. Your mother wants you, Ms. Ratcliff, and then I'm afraid the visitors need to leave. Our patient must have her rest."

Sandy and Mary were standing outside Linda's room. Pen came out, exchanging places with Rosalie. Her eyes were moist, the tip of her nose a little red. We said goodbye to everyone and headed down to the parking lot.

"I have the strongest feeling I've just seen my good friend for the last time," Pen said.

It was a valid premonition. Tuesday morning, Sandy and I were in her kitchen again when the call came. Linda had passed during the night.

Chapter 27

I'm afraid I can't get time away from the bank. Even though it's a death that hits so close for a dear friend, this doesn't fall under the bereavement rules. I feel rotten about that. Can you touch base with Pen during the day and see if she needs anything?"

"Of course. I'd be glad to."

I wasn't sure what I could offer that Pen's many friends in the valley couldn't handle better, but I was still determined to do what I could for Sophie and her mom. And that meant tracking various links to Eddie, which would hopefully lead me to Dixie. An anxious dread ran through me, a feeling that he might have harmed the mother, leaving the girl truly orphaned. I needed to follow through until I knew the answer.

Pen was my link to any possible inside information at

the police department, and I needed to keep that link open. Yesterday, we'd learned that Eddie died sometime between Thursday night and Friday morning, which brought back to mind the early predawn pounding on the door at the motel in Holbrook. Down inside, I'd harbored the thought that this might have been Eddie, looking for Sophie and, by extension, Dixie.

Now I realized the time frame made that difficult. From four a.m. Friday morning, for him to get back to Mesa would have been tight. Not impossible, but tight. I supposed he could have made the trip in less than the three hours it took us—traffic would have been light— and maybe he walked into Dixie's house and there was a confrontation. Scared out of her wits, she might have met him in the kitchen with that big old knife in her hand. Once he was lying there on the kitchen floor, she would have panicked and run.

So there was a certain logic to that scenario. And it made sense that she wouldn't be using her credit cards or phone. But motive? Other than an act of self-defense or crime of passion, it seemed much more logical that she could have gotten Eddie out of her life in less complicated ways.

Still, I had to admit that I didn't really know Dixie. Maybe she was the type who would act impetuously and then figure it all out later. In some ways that fit exactly with what I knew about her personality. I really needed to talk to her because her disappearance also sent me around in the circle where I had to admit the possibility that Eddie had harmed her first.

This thinking-in-a-loop got me through a breakfast of toast, a shower, and my preparations to get out the door and start the day. And for that I needed a plan.

I started with a condolence call to Rosalie. And, okay, I mixed in a little snooping.

After the routine "I'm so sorry" part of the conversation, I brought up Eddie and asked if she could expand upon what she'd started to tell me last night, about Eddie's gambling habits. In her search of her mother's records, had she come across the names of the casinos he frequented? Could she recall any buddies he hung out with?

She seemed to appreciate having a task. "It's better for me to keep busy," she said. "I just bagged up twenty-three bottles of medications that need to be disposed of. I'm tired of thinking about medical stuff. I'll get back to you."

It had only taken me two days in this huge city to learn that you wait until after nine o'clock if you don't want to be sitting at a standstill in morning rush hour traffic. By the time I put the breakfast things in Sandy's dishwasher and gathered my purse and a light jacket, it was close enough. I headed for Pen's Scottsdale home.

"I tried to sit down with my latest manuscript," she said after she ushered me in and offered tea. "Simply could not concentrate well enough to write a halfway good scene. I admire those writers who turn out pages every single day, no matter what else is going on in their lives. I suspect those are the ones who have to go back and perform major edits on shoddy work."

"It's not a crime to take some time for yourself." I accepted tea in a delicate china cup that probably came from England.

"I know. My readers are a very understanding group." She pointed out the sugar and milk, in case I wanted some. "I did hear from Benton again this morning. He called to offer his sympathy about Linda, and he also said he'd picked up an interesting tidbit from the current D.A."

We took seats on a beautiful white couch and I waited for her to continue.

"It seems that in the search for Edward Peppard's next of kin, they've come up with a son, but they haven't yet located him."

"Did we know anything about that? Sophie sure didn't say anything."

"I believe this is a big surprise, although I should phone Rosalie and verify. I'm certain Linda never mentioned Edward having any children."

"What else did Benton say—any other information about this son? His name?"

"He did give me the name and his last known address. Apparently, the medical examiner's office wants instructions from the next of kin, in order to release the body. If no one comes along—I suspect this means someone willing to take on the expenses of burial and all that—they will release the body to the state and he'll get some type of generic burial, no service of any type."

"Well, surely they'll reach this son quickly enough. I would like the name, though. He may have information that could help identify Eddie's enemies, someone who is a more likely killer than Dixie." Maybe the son himself had a major beef with his dad.

Pen stood up and walked to her kitchen counter, where she picked up a small notepad. "This is what I wrote down as I was talking to Benton. The boy's name is Alex. Born Alexander Peppard, although he also goes by Alex Planchard. He has an address in Fountain Hills, but apparently has not been there recently. At least the police have not located him there."

"How old? You said he's a boy?"

Pen laughed. "At my age, everyone is youthful. Apparently he's old enough that he doesn't live with his parents, but that's about all I can tell you."

"I could check with my brother in Albuquerque. He runs background checks on people as a big part of our business. He might get a little picky about having the person's authorization to dig very far, though."

"Oh, that's all right. You'll recall that we have someone on our team with no such compunction about looking into a person's details. Especially if that person is on the wrong side of the law."

We didn't know that about Eddie's son, but I wasn't going to quibble. Anything that would lead me to Dixie O'Connell quicker was fine in my book.

Pen glanced at an elegant wristwatch. "It's early evening in Spain, and Amber is most likely either enjoying tapas at some little streetside bar or she's home at her computer. Shall we make a bet?"

She won, guessing it would be the computer. Pen placed her phone on speaker and we outlined the basics of our query. I could hear keys tapping rapidly in the background.

"Yeah, the Fountain Hills address is a few months old. His credit report shows an application for an upscale condo complex in Scottsdale." Amber gave an address, and Pen immediately knew where it was, near the popular Fashion Square. "Sounds like he came into some money."

"Or he planned to," I offered.

"Give me a few more hours and I'll see what other background info I can find." Our young colleague sounded excited at having a new quest.

I added Alexander Peppard's alias, and his address and phone number, provided by Amber, to my contacts. It could be an interesting meeting. I was about to leave Pen's place and head over to his condo, figuring a face-to-face would beat a phone call from a stranger, when my phone rang and I saw it was Rosalie.

"I'm hoping this will be helpful," I said to Pen as I picked up the phone.

"Charlie, Rosalie Ratcliff here. I found some names for you. Ready to take them down?"

I borrowed a sheet from Pen's notepad and wrote everything she told me. Two different casinos, both on Native American land near the fringes of the city. "Most of Mother's rolodex is filled with cards in her writing, some even in my dad's, but here are two names, both written in Edward's handwriting."

I took those as well, although I had a hard time believing he wouldn't have simply entered his own contacts into his phone, rather than committing them to a card and leaving a paper trail. Most likely they were something he wanted Linda to have, a plumber or auto mechanic or someone like that. But I could follow through and see what I came up with.

"Rosalie, I just learned something interesting since I last spoke with you … Eddie had a son named Alexander. Alex. You hadn't mentioned him so I wondered—"

"A son? Seriously? No, I'd *never* heard this. I'd be willing to swear that Mother hadn't either. She never said a thing about this Alex."

She sounded so genuinely flummoxed that I believed her.

Chapter 28

I hung up from the call with Rosalie and turned to Pen. "Do you mind if I stay a few more minutes and make some calls?"

"Of course, do." She offered more tea but I passed it up.

The first name Rosalie had given was Jorge Gadiz, listed in her rolodex with the business name ABC Enterprises. How much more generic could you get? I decided on my approach and tapped in the number.

A gruff male voice answered with, "Yeah?"

"Um, my mother had you listed in her address book as a plumber?"

"Who's your mother?"

I wasn't going down that path. "Maybe she meant electrician. Is that what ABC Enterprises does?"

"You got the wrong number, lady." The call went dead.

Okay, so my approach had been a stupid one. I dialed the other number, the one for a Chaco Kaynor.

"Valley Pawn," said a female voice.

"I'm calling for Eddie Peppard."

There was some shuffling and muttered words and a man came on the line. "Eddie Peppard ain't here. Who's this?"

I hit the red button and ended the call quickly. I'd already learned a lot. I looked up Valley Pawn and found their address, right across the road from one of the casinos Rosalie had named. This could not be a coincidence.

I gathered my notes, phone, and purse and turned to Pen. "I'm going to go by the condo where we think Alex is living, then I'll probably be heading for the casinos. Want to come along?"

She gave a light laugh. "Oh, my dear, I'm afraid that is an environment where I do not fit at all. I've only been inside one American casino in my life and it was readily apparent I did not belong."

I'm no casino regular myself, and I knew what she meant. With her expensive haircut, flawless skin, cashmere and wool designer clothing … no. Pen was definitely not going to blend in. I would go it alone.

I'd always pictured Scottsdale as a somewhat sleepy little enclave of the ultra rich, nestled into the foothills somewhat above the fray of the surrounding metro area. But the neighborhood around Fashion Square was anything but tranquil. Addresses weren't easy to spot, and I ended up circling the high-end mall a couple of times before I spotted the entrance to the condo complex where Alex had qualified to rent one of the million-dollar places.

Amber's address information had included the unit number, although it was no easy feat to simply take the elevator there. A doorman stood guard at the heavy glass double doors to the lobby, which smelled of fresh flowers and money. A concierge of some sort looked up at me with that raised-eyebrow, drawn-mouth expression meant to convey he was every bit as wealthy as the residents. For all I knew maybe he was.

"May I help you?"

I should have thought this through. All I could come up with was to give my name and say I was here to see Alex Planchard.

"Is he expecting you?"

Is that any of your business? I didn't actually say it, but I wanted to. "It's regarding Linda Ratcliff." Was it dumb of me to say that? Maybe. But if his father's money-grubbing influence was present in the son, I imagined dropping the name of the wealthy widow might open the door.

The concierge picked up a desk phone, exchanged a few quiet words with someone, hung up the receiver, and looked back at me. "I'm sorry. His housekeeper informs me he is presently not at home."

Right. In any ordinary neighborhood, this challenge would only lead me to sneak around to the back door and find a way. That wasn't going to cut it here. I was beginning to understand why the locals called this town Snotsdale.

I slunk back to my rented Highlander, easily the cheapest vehicle in the region, and waited with an eye on the exit from the building's parking garage. But since I had only a vague idea of what Alex looked like and no idea what he drove, it soon became apparent this was a complete waste of time. I was just about to drive away, having decided to check in with Gracie and Sophie, when I spotted a semi-familiar government car. Detective Hernandez parked at the curb and stepped out.

I was *so* tempted to follow him, to see if he would get the same story from the concierge, but that wouldn't get me up to the condo, nor would it most likely gain me any information. I waited until the cop was inside the building before I got out of my vehicle and crossed the street. I found a spot where I could watch the front doors without being pegged by the doorman as a stalker.

Five minutes later, when Hernandez approached his car, I carefully contrived to accidentally bump into him.

"Oh! Sorry."

"Charlie Parker." He said it in the exact same tone Kent Taylor tends to use when he sees me. Sheesh, what is it with cops? Am I exuding some kind of repellant pheromone?

I put on a sweet smile and asked how his day was going.

"We can't both be at this address at the same time by accident," he said.

"Well …"

"I know you came in asking to see Alex Peppard aka Planchard. The concierge told me."

The rat. I snapped my mouth shut to keep from saying it out loud.

"I'm warning you, Ms. Parker, to stay away from my murder investigation."

"Detective, I'm not even *trying* to get into your murder case, believe me. I'm here in the city to reunite a runaway girl with her mother. The mother has a connection to this Alex person, as I'm sure you know, and that's where *my* investigation was going." It was mostly true.

"You told the desk guy you were here about Linda Ratcliff."

Wow. Thorough. "She passed away last night. I thought

Alex might want to know."

Hernandez looked surprised by this news, and I felt a tiny surge of triumph at being ahead of him in one small thing. I decided to press my luck.

"You weren't in there very long. Did 'the housekeeper' also tell you Alex was out?"

"Yeah, that was the story."

"Did you believe it?"

He gave a shrug. "I think that desk guy is probably paid a lot of money to convey whatever information he's told."

I didn't have a snappy comeback since I agreed with him. Something about the exchange had made me question whether it was actually Alex telling the guy to brush me off. Now the detective's response gave me the same impression. Hernandez put his hand on the door handle of his sedan, a clear sign that he was finished with me.

"Can I ask one more question?" I hoped my winsome smile would work.

"What's that?"

"Do you know where Dixie O'Connell is, and is she a suspect in your case?"

"Technically, that's two questions." But there was a hint of mirth beneath his scowl. "No, and yes."

He opened the door. "And, Ms. Parker? If you discover the answer to your first question, I expect you to let me know."

I nodded to give him the impression I would comply. We'd have to see how it actually went before I would commit to turning Dixie over.

Hernandez got into his car but made no move to start it. It looked as though he planned to do just what I'd thought of, watch the exit and see if Alex left the building.

Odds were, he had a photo of the young man and knew who he was looking for, something I did not have. He sent a sharp glance in my direction, which meant *go away*. Since I couldn't very well hang out on the sidewalk for hours, and sitting across the street in my vehicle wasn't going to win points with the detective, I decided it was in my own best interest to leave the surveillance to the pro. I could find better things to do with my time.

I turned right at the next intersection and pulled into a Starbucks where I could plan my next moves.

Chapter 29

While my latte was being prepared, I phoned Gracie. "How's everything going today?"

"I forget what's it's like to have a kid who's not in school. My plan to run around and pick up everything for Thanksgiving dinner is now combined with a trip to the mall for shoes."

"Shoes?"

"Yeah, she's trying on stuff now. The red cowboy boots are cute as all get-out, but I started noticing black scuffs on my tile floors so I had to ask her to remove them indoors. Not to mention, she had nothing warm to put on her feet in the early mornings. Said she'd put on the boots in Santa Fe and must have just forgotten to pack her regular shoes. So, we're looking for trainers and slippers."

For me, that would be a ten-minute stop somewhere

quick and easy.

"Are all girls this picky about their footwear? Mine certainly hasn't reached that stage yet. Hoping she doesn't." To someone in the distance, she said, "Those are really cute. How about those?"

I told Gracie about Linda's death, something she'd already heard from Sandy. Then I briefed her on the discovery that Eddie Peppard had a son, and the background work Amber had discovered for us.

"I had no luck at his condo, so I'm thinking about what to do next. Would it be possible for me to grab Sophie's attention long enough to ask her a couple things?"

"Probably. I'm thinking—hoping—we've got the shoe decisions nailed down." An exchange went on, during which Gracie told Sophie to talk to me while she took the shoes and paid for them.

"Hey, Charlie, did Gracie tell you about our shopping trip?"

A little polite chatter and then I got down to the real reason for my call, asking about Eddie's son Alex.

"A grown son? No, I swear he never said anything about that around me. And I'm pretty sure Mom didn't know either. She would have said something."

"How about these two names—Jorge Gadiz? Chaco Kaynor?"

"Ummm, not sure … I think there was a Jorge he mentioned a time or two. Some kind of business associate."

"Did he say what kind of business?"

"Not really. One time I was home, like, all alone and there was a call on the landline, from some casino person who wanted to talk to Mr. Peppard. They didn't want to leave a message so I never wrote it down or anything."

"Was it Sculpted Rock, or Misty Mountain?"

"Yeah, probably something like that. I don't know …"

"But you got the impression this casino and Jorge Gadiz were connected somehow?"

"I suppose. I mean, the person on the phone wasn't this Jorge guy. It was a woman."

"Did you mention the call to Eddie?"

"Shit, no. Sorry. No. By that time him and me weren't getting along at all."

I remembered the texts I'd seen on Sophie's phone, where she was accusing Eddie of gambling and seeing other women.

Something about the background sounds changed, and I pictured Gracie, having culminated the shoe purchase, herding her young charge out to the car to get on with their errands. I thanked Sophie for the information, got back on the line with Gracie just long enough to wish her a nice day. She repeated her invitation for me to join her family for Thanksgiving dinner. I stayed vague, wanting to think I wouldn't still be in Arizona two days from now.

On that note, I took my latte to a table and looked up the directions to the Misty Mountain Casino. Their website took me through a series of pages to introduce me to their "team." Apparently companies don't merely have employees anymore. I didn't spot either Jorge Gadiz or Chaco Kaynor among the mid- to upper-level management.

A trip to the site of the other, Sculpted Rock Casino, did net a tidbit. Jorge Gadiz was listed as a management-level security officer, which I discovered on another page is someone who walks the casino floor and watches for cheaters and scammers. Since Eddie was both of those things, it could be a friendship made in heaven if Gadiz was willing to look the other way or accept a few pennies in return for … whatever.

I zoomed out on the map and discovered a reminder of something I'd seen earlier. Valley Pawn sat across the street from the big casino. The pawn shop was where I had called to locate Chaco Kaynor. Suddenly it seemed both of Eddie's business associates just happened to be in close proximity to each other. How nice and cozy that seemed.

I could head north in that direction right now. Except my phone chimed at that very moment. I saw Rosalie's name on the screen.

"I told you I couldn't sit still," she began. "It's way too quiet to sit around, thinking."

"Do you need help with funeral arrangements or anything?" I didn't mean to make it sound like an offer to drop what I was doing, but I really felt for her.

"Oh, no. Nothing like that. Mother had enough advance warning that she'd said goodbye to all her friends. She asked for a simple cremation and no memorial service, so there's really nothing to plan. Well-meaning friends have dropped food by for me, but I'm donating most of it to the homeless shelter. One person can only consume so many chicken casseroles and vanilla Bundt cakes. I've decided to spend the time going through Mother's finances in preparation for dealing with her estate, and that's what I'm calling about. You're an accountant, right?"

"Yes, but one with no experience in estates."

"My questions aren't specific to that. I'm running into some anomalies in her investment accounts. I wonder if an experienced person could take a look and tell me what some of these things mean?"

"Did she have an accountant?"

"Yes, but with the end of the year coming up, he's

bogged down with his many corporate clients and isn't booking any appointments until well after the first of the year. What I'm looking at may be nothing for concern …"

"No problem. What part of the city are you in?"

She told me and, although it was not exactly close, I figured I could get there shortly after noon and still break away to cross the valley again before the afternoon rush started around three p.m. What a pain for those who lived here—plan the entire day around staying out of traffic, or jump right in and join the craziness. I told her to expect me within an hour or so.

When I arrived, Rosalie led me into Linda's living room, tastefully done in furnishings that were top-notch twenty-five years ago. The white sofa, blue armchairs, Oriental rugs, and understated silk floral arrangements had been immaculately kept and were actually much more tasteful than most of the modern trends I'd spotted in recent years.

We passed through to the dining room, where the table was covered with the contents of some file folders.

"These are the brokerage statements for the last year," she told me. "If I'm understanding them correctly, all these transactions seem to be transfers completed online."

I took the sheet she handed me and looked it over. "Seems that way. There are some fairly large amounts." I was seeing several in the five-figure range, and each of the last two months showed a couple of six-figure transactions.

"I know. Mother never said anything about needing that much money from her investments. There were medical bills, of course, but she had excellent health insurance. Her out-of-pocket costs would have been nothing close to this."

I glanced at another sheet from the previous year. "I'm

not seeing such large transfers last year."

"No. And look at this." She pointed to the notation on one transaction fourteen months ago. "Phone authorization, and then a bunch of numbers. That would be more Mother's style. She would call the brokerage to tell them what she wanted to do. She never quite came to trust online banking."

"When did the online transactions begin? Maybe once she got sick it was easier to handle it that way, rather than timing her calls to the office hours of the firm?"

Rosalie stared at the pile of statements. "I'd have to go through them all."

"Can I ask you straight out—do you think this was Eddie's doing? Either he pushed her to modernize her methods or he somehow got into her accounts?"

"That has definitely crossed my mind, Charlie. I—I just didn't want to think—" She paced to the far end of the room and back. "I wanted to think Mother was with it enough not to let herself get scammed. It makes me so sad to see the extent of this."

"How computer literate was Eddie? Did he have enough information to set up online access? A person usually has to have quite a bit of background on someone in order to convince any fiduciary institution."

She waved her arm to encompass all the paperwork. "Everything is probably somewhere here in this house. All he would need to do is dig around."

Easy enough to accomplish while Linda was away at her medical appointments or with Rosalie or friends. It would take a lot more time and skill than I could give it, just to dig far enough to learn where Eddie had stashed Linda's money. Then the procedure would be to turn it over to law enforcement and hope to prosecute and recover the funds. Except now Eddie was dead.

Chapter 30

Rosalie and I sat down with the statements and a calculator and added up the various online transactions, going backward from the present time to the point where they began. There was nearly a half-million dollars gone, and the account to which the transfers had been made was not one of Linda's.

"You'll want to call the brokerage and find out identifying information for the account that received the funds. Maybe they can give some guidance on the best step forward, as far as prosecuting or retrieving your mother's money."

She looked completely overwhelmed at the thought.

"It doesn't need to be done right away. Notify them in writing of your mother's death. That's a first step. At least no one can impersonate her online and move more money."

She nodded. "I'm having to notify dozens, every place from the electric company to the banks to her favorite charities who are sending their year-end donation requests. This will be just one more."

A glance at my watch told me I hadn't managed to avoid the traffic, but I could work that out. Rosalie walked me to the front door. "Thank you for your help, Charlie. This whole job is daunting."

"This is probably a silly question, but have you come across any list of passwords or that type of information maintained by Eddie? To keep track of his own affairs, plus setting things up in Linda's name … It would have been more than he'd want to remember, I'm guessing." What I really hoped to find, I must admit, was whether he was targeting Dixie in a similar way.

"Nothing like that. In fact, the more I think about it, I never knew Eddie to be much into computers and such. He had a smart phone. That was about it. Of course, he could have probably done all sorts of things with that, or by using Mother's computer. She only used it for emails and storing her photos, and the machine is terribly outdated."

"Add it to your list of things to check. The browser history could tell you a lot." I had to be careful not to jump right in and volunteer to do it for her. "If you come across a bunch of passwords, let me know if anything doesn't look at all familiar. It's highly possible that Dixie O'Connell is another of his victims, and I'd love to know if Eddie used your mother's computer to set up accounts from which he scammed both women."

I said goodbye and headed to the Highlander, which I'd parked in her driveway. The sun was already dipping low in the west, a fiery orange ball nearing the horizon. I drove a block or so away, just so Rosalie wouldn't think I was lurking, and pulled to the curb to make some calls.

Sandy told me not to worry about getting to her place for dinner. With all that was going on, she was deliberately keeping things casual. Next, I checked in with Gracie, but there was nothing new to report there. Sophie still had heard nothing from her mother.

With that worrying at me, I decided to head out to the Sculpted Rock Casino and see if Jorge Gadiz was on duty. It was possible that Eddie had taken Dixie there, may have introduced the fun-loving young woman to Jorge, and perhaps the man could give me some clues. If I got really lucky, maybe I'd find Dixie out there herself, partying it up.

I reminded myself not to wish for that, though. If I found her that way, it would mean she really was the bad mother of the year, and poor Sophie didn't have much of a life to look forward to. Neither scenario—Dixie partying or Dixie missing—was a good one.

Sculpted Rock, with its brightly lit parking lot and neon trim around the art deco style building, was easy to spot as the evening sky grew darker in contrast. The parking lot was less than a third full. I chalked it up to this being a Tuesday, early in the evening, and prior to a holiday weekend. I walked inside to find that, no matter what you'd think from the outside, a casino is a noisy place inside with all the bells, beeps, and electronic chatter from the slot machines.

A wave of fatigue hit me and I realized my breakfast toast had worn off long ago. I should have stopped for something to eat before I got here. My hunger, combined with the frenzied racket all around me, sent me frantically looking for a way to get off the central casino floor. In one corner I spotted a cluster of signs and I walked toward them.

There was a dressed-up convenience store, the kind with tiny packets of aspirin for six dollars and a variety of touristy items to proclaim that you'd spent time at Sculpted Rock. A second shop's windows showed off high-end clothing in case a woman needed to dress up to stick money into a slot machine. But I smelled food. Bennie's Roadhouse looked like a casual café, while The Grill seemed like a steakhouse complete with an upscale wine menu. I opted for Bennie's.

The small space was set up cafeteria style and it was buzzing with the early crowd, a big portion of whom were casino employees taking their dinner break. I joined the line and studied the menu on the wall, deciding a turkey sandwich would work just fine. By the time I filled my little tray with the sandwich, some chips, and a caffeinated fountain soda, I looked around to find that all the tables were full. A young woman sitting at a two-place high table noticed my predicament and waved me over.

"It always gets a little crazy in here right about this time. I often bring my own lunch and eat in the employee lounge, but today kind of got away from me." Her name badge said S. Tozzi.

I laughed as I set my tray down and settled into the seat across from her. "Me too. I'm actually working now, but didn't want to faint right in front of the security manager."

"Oh, you're here to see Jorge? Looking for a job?"

"Yes to talking with Jorge, no to looking for a job."

"He's around here somewhere tonight. I saw him around mid-afternoon. I'm Stella, by the way."

"I understand Jorge was a friend of Eddie Peppard," I

mentioned as I unwrapped my sandwich. "And Eddie was a regular around here."

"Oh yeah. I'm surprised he hasn't been by in several days now."

I delivered the bad news.

Stella looked up, her plastic fork dropping into her salad bowl. "Oh my gosh. I hadn't heard. What happened?"

I switched directions, rather than get in trouble with Hernandez for talking about the murder scene. "I take it Eddie was the friendly sort, with everyone around here?"

"Oh, life of the party Eddie. I suppose I had more contact with him than some others. I'm a cashier, and he was at my window a lot in recent weeks, paying down his account, which had run up kind of high."

"So, players are allowed to establish an account here?"

"Some. Very few. But Eddie was an old friend of Jorge's from way back. That's my impression anyway. Jorge puts a good word in with the general manager and his friends pretty much get what they want. Up to a point—I think there's a $25,000 limit on open credit."

That was way less than I'd seen on the statements Rosalie showed me, but it could account for some of the casino spending. I decided to press my advantage a little further. "I recently met Eddie's lady friend, Linda. She seemed to be supporting his gambling. Maybe she was giving him the money."

"Linda? I don't remember a Linda. Sounds older. He was in the casino a lot with a younger woman with a cute-ish name. Trixie?"

"Dixie?"

"Yeah, yeah that's it! She'd hang around with him at the craps table, but I mainly remember her coming in every time we had a band. There's a big amphitheater out back—part of the casino property. Every time there was a concert, Dixie wanted to come. From Eddie, I kind of got the impression he didn't care much about the music. He'd get, like, front-row seats and park her out there, then he'd come in and get into a poker game or something for a couple hours."

"Have you seen her in the last few days? With or without Eddie?"

Stella shook her head. "Nope." She glanced at her phone screen. "I gotta get back to work. Break time's over."

I thanked her for sharing her table. "Sorry I was the bearer of the bad news about Eddie."

She nodded solemnly and drifted away. I watched through the café window as she threaded her way between tables and stopped beside a man in a pale gray business suit. I recognized Jorge Gadiz, who looked just like his online employee photo. Whatever she said to him, he reacted with a somber nod. He already knew about Eddie's death. He gave her a pat on the shoulder and she walked on.

I crunched down on a potato chip and thought about the conversation. I'd probably learned just as much from Stella the cashier as I would get out of Gadiz, but it couldn't hurt to speak with him anyway. I knew where to find him now. I finished my little dinner and left the café in search of my next interview.

Gadiz was nowhere to be seen among the gaming tables so I trekked through the rows of noisy slot machines. Didn't spot him there either. I walked to the cashier area, against the back wall of the large space, thinking I could ask Stella where I might find the manager. From that angle, a glance upward showed me a mezzanine with a cozy bar above the high-end roulette and poker tables.

Seated on barstools were Jorge Gadiz and a familiar woman; both sat in profile to me. The bright blonde hair caught my eye; the short dress with thin straps which showed off her deeply tanned arms and legs confirmed it. She sat facing Jorge, laughing, clearly flirting. It was Carleen from the dog rescue, Dixie's coworker. Interesting.

She hadn't mentioned gambling, but now the casino seemed to be another connection with Eddie. Seeing Carleen here with Gadiz gave me another possible suspect for my list. I stood at a slot machine, trying to look interested in it while sneaking peeks up at the mezzanine bar. A hulk-sized man in a dark business suit approached Gadiz, stooped to say something into his ear. After Gadiz responded, the other man walked away. He stared for a moment down at the casino floor and I tried my best to look like a happy gambler.

I debated going up to the mezzanine and walking right up to Carleen and Gadiz, but what would I say? Both knew Eddie was dead. Neither was likely to admit any involvement in that. I'd already asked Carleen if she knew where Dixie was, and the odds were by this time Gadiz also knew I was looking for her.

Stella the cashier had said Dixie had not been around in recent days. Logic told me it was unlikely Dixie would come here, or to any of Eddie's known hangouts, right after his murder. The police always track down the victim's interests and look for connections. In fact, I wouldn't be surprised to see Hernandez come waltzing in here, questioning all who had known the victim.

Discouragement swept over me. It was my sixth day since picking up Sophie and I felt no closer to delivering her to her mom than at the beginning. I decided it was time to leave the casino, maybe even to leave Phoenix. Unless a good night's sleep changed my outlook, I was ready to give up the hunt for Dixie O'Connell and let the authorities handle Sophie. I pulled my keys from my purse and made for the wide glass exit doors.

It was fully dark out now, except for the rosy glow of the city in the background. I'd almost reached the Highlander when a scuff sounded on the asphalt behind me. I whirled, instinctively gripping the keys between my fingers, every hair on my body standing on end.

Chapter 31

Quit asking around about Eddie Peppard," came a deep voice to my left. It was the hulk who'd spoken to Gadiz in the bar, not even ten minutes ago.

A second man, smaller but somehow more deadly looking, stood to my right, cracking his knuckles. His expression was eerily bland.

"I-I-I'm not trying—"

Dark-suit cut me off. "Just leave it. Things happen for a reason."

The second man spoke, his voice barely above a whisper. "Women alone in the dark sometimes get hurt." He took a step backward, and the two men blended away into the shadows at the side of the building.

I jumped into my SUV and locked the doors. Okay, that did it. I started the engine and beat it the hell out of that parking lot. I was five blocks away before my heartbeat slowed enough so I wasn't hearing it pounding in my ears.

The longer I drove, the madder I got. *I'm not here to ruin their gambling operation, or loan sharking or whatever was going on with Eddie and his gambling habits, his other women, or anything else.* But now I knew—I couldn't walk away from Sophie, not without knowing that her mom was okay. Especially now, after the veiled threat about women alone in the dark.

I found a well-lit shopping center and pulled in near a huge supermarket that had plenty of people walking in and out. Pulling up the number for Detective Hernandez, I reported everything that had just happened, including names and descriptions. I kind of ignored his question about what I'd been doing at the casino in the first place.

He said they were well aware of Edward Peppard's gambling and his habit of running up debt, but he didn't share a whole lot beyond that. Nonetheless, I breathed a lot easier after the conversation.

There was one other thread I'd intended to follow and I was still in the part of the city to do it. I pulled out of the supermarket lot and backtracked toward the casino.

Chaco Kaynor. When I'd called Kaynor's number, the phone was answered with, "Valley Pawn," and it was too nearby for me to ignore. I drove past it once and had to circle back, realizing belatedly that it was just a small shop in an unimpressive little strip mall, along with a Laundromat, a Mexican restaurant, a Pack & Ship, and a barber shop. At this hour, the only ones open were the laundry and the restaurant. Both were hopping.

I parked among the crowd at the laundry, got out, and walked next door past the front window of the pawn shop, pretending to admire the wares beyond the iron bars. The good stuff such as jewelry—if they had any—must have been locked away in the big safe that was visible by soft night lighting at the back of the shop. Hm, what next?

I strolled back to the laundry and went inside. Two women were folding clothes at some big tables, and a man was reading a magazine. No one paid any attention to me as I located a back door and stepped out. The alley behind the long building was asphalt paved and lined with dumpsters, one for each business.

At the far end of the building someone stepped out the back door of the restaurant and tipped a bin into their dumpster, shook it a couple of times, and went back inside. They never even looked in my direction. I scoped out the back door of the pawn shop. It was metal, with a welded piece that prevented someone from inserting a screwdriver or blade to jimmy the door. The oblong small window was woven with metal wire of some kind. Stickers proclaimed the presence of an alarm system, but they were old and faded and I didn't see any sign of contact points, cameras, or a panel. Was I willing to chance it, even if I could figure out a way through the heavy door?

While I was debating my options, a car pulled into the alley, coming from the far end by the restaurant. I ducked behind the laundry's dumpster, which held the oddly comforting scent of fabric softener sheets, expecting the car to drive on past. It didn't. It stopped exactly where I'd been standing twenty-five seconds ago.

One of the doors opened and someone got out. "Keep an eye on the back seat," said a gruff male voice.

"She's totally out of it," a woman whined. "I want to come in and see the new necklace you were telling me about."

"I'll grab that for you."

The car door slammed. I wanted to take a peek but the headlights were on and the engine running. Keys jingled, the guy opened a lock, and I heard the tiny electronic beeps of numbers on a keypad. So there was a working alarm system after all. I made myself small in the shadow of the dumpster and waited.

I swore an hour passed, but it was more likely around ten minutes before the pawnshop door opened and closed again. I felt my ankles starting to cramp up. When the car door opened, I heard the same man's voice. "There, don't ever say I didn't give nothin' nice to my pretty little Carleen."

The door slammed and I missed out on her reaction to what I assumed was the jewelry she'd mentioned. I was still processing the quick verbal exchange when the car wheeled around the dumpster and passed me. I saw that it was a dark Suburban; I got most of the license plate and began repeating it in my head.

Once the vehicle turned out of sight, I grabbed my phone from my purse and dictated the letters and numbers into a note. Only when that information was safely stored did I allow myself to parse the words and sort out the details.

He'd clearly used the name Carleen. So … she was in the casino half an hour ago, flirting like crazy with Jorge Gadiz. Was he the owner of the pawnshop? I didn't think so.

I unfolded myself from my hiding spot beside the dumpster, wincing at the pain in my feet and hips. Sheesh, am I really getting that old and creaky? As I walked around the end of the laundry building and back to my car, I convinced myself that it wasn't age. I was really dead tired and still at least a half hour from my warm bed at Sandy's house. I headed in that direction, hoping in my exhausted state I didn't miss a crucial turn or two.

"Did you have your radio on in the car?" Sandy asked when I walked in.

"No, why?"

"They're saying a big winter storm is passing through the northern part of the state. Interstate 40 is closed from Flagstaff to Albuquerque. It's a good thing you didn't try to go home today."

I had to agree. But now the question was whether I'd be able to get out tomorrow. And on the Wednesday before Thanksgiving, even if I could leave, the holiday traffic would be murder.

Sandy seemed curious about my day but I had to admit I was too flat-out tired to hold my eyes open another minute, much less talk. She took pity and brewed me a cup of bedtime tea to carry into the bedroom with me. I didn't even manage three sips of it before I was out.

But my sleep was restless, filled with the dozens of conversations from the previous day, all blending into a nonsensical mess. At some point I realized I didn't know whether we had heard from Amber all day. Some unanswered question hung at the edge of my consciousness but I couldn't bring it to mind. I let the darkness of sleep overtake me again.

Chapter 32

I woke up refreshed, still torn between staying to help find Dixie O'Connell and my determination to get back to Albuquerque today. Then I remembered they'd closed the interstate last night. I sat up in Sandy's plushy, comfy guest bed and picked up my phone to check the situation. The news coverage sounded dire—stranded vehicles, dramatic rescues, overflowing motels and truck stops where travelers had fled for shelter, videos showing a foot of snow.

Okay, that was last night, as Drake would remind me. I needed to know what the future held. Luckily, my piloting experience had taught me how to read a weather map. I bypassed the news channels with their perky meteorologists and went straight to the aviation weather charts. The storm was a fast-moving one, and it had already passed through Arizona and most of New Mexico. The cold-front trajectory showed it heading with a vengeance toward Texas and Oklahoma. That was the good news—well, from my perspective. The sky was clear now and there wasn't another storm moving onto my horizon for several more days.

The highway department reports told the rest of the story. Plows were out, doing their best to clear the major highways, but with many vehicles stuck and a couple of sideways semi-trucks, it would be slow going. Drivers were advised not to travel except in emergency situations. My mood plummeted. Wasn't getting home before the turkey was gone considered an emergency?

Adapt, Charlie. It ain't over 'til it's over.

And, there was still a mystery to solve. I washed my face and brushed my teeth and put on a pair of fresh jeans and one of my new sweaters before joining Sandy in the kitchen.

"It's still early," she said. "Did you get enough sleep?"

I hadn't even noticed the time on my phone. The digital clock on her microwave told me it was 6:24 and a glance toward the window showed it was still dark outside.

"I guess I did. I woke up feeling perky and ready to hit the road, except it looks like that's not going to happen because of the weather. Maybe later in the day." I accepted the mug of coffee she handed me.

"Well, the bank is open until three o'clock today, so I'm on my regular schedule. I'm glad you're up. I wanted to tell you about my call with Amber yesterday." She bustled around the kitchen, making toast and breaking eggs into a bowl, as she talked.

"Oh good. I was wondering if she found anything useful for us."

"It was interesting, let's just say. Pen and Rosalie were

in on the call, and Amber was able to somehow get access to Linda's computer remotely. I still don't have a clue how that works, but I guess it does."

I added a little cream to my coffee and encouraged her to go on.

"She found the various money transfers out of Linda's accounts and said she has enough data to start tracing where it went. Personally, I'm expecting that to be straight to Edward Peppard. But if she can get his account numbers, she says there's a chance she can transfer it back out. Whatever remains."

She handed me a plate of scrambled eggs covered in shredded cheese and salsa, and a slice of toast. We took seats at the counter.

"I wouldn't hold out hope to recover much. I talked with a cashier at Eddie's favorite casino last night. She didn't give figures but said he'd paid down his debts significantly in the last few weeks."

The eggs were delicious and I made a good dent in my breakfast before I remembered something else.

"I visited that pawn shop, the one where they answered the number I was given for Eddie's buddy Chaco. The place was closed but someone came along. I got a license number. Do you think Amber can trace that for me?"

"Ask her. It's only three in the afternoon where she is. You have her number, right?"

I could see that Sandy was feeling a little pressured to finish getting ready for work, so I assured her I would follow through with Amber and the other Heist Ladies, and I would clean up the kitchen.

Once she was out the door, I helped myself to another cup of coffee and placed the video call to Amber. She looked a little bleary this morning, her dusky cocoa skin a bit pasty and her wild curls sticking out at angles. She noticed that I'd noticed.

"I'm getting a late start today," she said with a wan smile. "Pulled an all-nighter digging for the information on Linda Ratcliff's accounts."

"Oh gosh, I don't think the Ladies realized what time it must have been for you in Europe."

"It's fine. I'm the original night owl. So, you're still at Sandy's house?"

"I am. She left for work, but she told me about last night's call, that you'd done a great job tracking Linda's money."

"Well, I hope so. I was able to get specifics on the money that moved out, but finding where it is now, that's another thing. It appears to have gone to some kind of shell corporation offshore. From there … I'm still working on that."

"I'm surprised. I got the impression that Eddie wasn't all that computer literate. I pictured him more as a cash-in-hand kind of guy."

"Oh, this isn't Eddie we're talking about. It's his son, Alex."

"Whoa …"

"Yeah. He's twenty-one years old and I'd say he's among the best in the hacking world. I'm actually a little in awe of his skills. He'd completely taken over Linda's computer, and with her passwords, which Eddie probably supplied, he managed her finances right into the Peppard family pockets."

"No kidding!"

"I found at least three layers of shell corporations

where he sent money zipping through a variety of servers in other countries."

"Is he doing this from abroad somewhere?"

"Nope, right there in the Phoenix area."

I remembered the Scottsdale condo. "I'll stick with this until I catch up with him."

"I know nothing about him personally, but his father hung out with some rough types. Alex's meanness may go beyond what he can do with a computer, so watch yourself."

"That reminds me. I have an Arizona vehicle plate number. Can you trace that and find out who owns it? In a dark alley last night I only noticed it was large and dark, probably a black Suburban."

"I'm on it. Might take me an hour or two?"

"That's fine. Just text me the info when you get it. I'm going to follow up some other threads here today."

She gave a big grin. "I like it that you said 'when' not 'if.'"

"Hey, you've demonstrated to me how sharp you are."

"If one of your threads is to track down Alex Peppard or Planchard or whatever name he uses there, just be careful," she repeated. "He's sharp and I think he's on to the fact that I've tracked his banking moves."

"Seriously?"

"He may not know it's me, but he knows someone's looking. I've found tracking cookies where there should be none. I erased them and switched servers, but yeah. I'm dead serious."

Chapter 33

Before the call with Amber even ended, I began thinking about Dixie. Was Eddie pulling this same thing with her, draining away the money left to her to raise Sophie? I needed more information so I could put Amber on that trail. I called Gracie.

"Oh yeah, our household is all awake. My kids have a half-day at school today but it'll be nothing serious. A bunch of the parents have pulled their kids out so they can travel."

"Up north doesn't look great for a road trip."

"No, and the airports throughout the Midwest are all in a tangle." Something clattered in the background. "Sophie and I are here, peeling and boiling potatoes, hoping she'll hear from her mother."

"So there's been nothing from Dixie?"

"Nada."

"Can I talk to Sophie? I just got off the phone with Amber and I thought of a lead we might have her follow."

She handed over the phone and I asked Sophie how she was doing. Received a *meh* sort of noise in response. I actually felt for her. None of this was going the way she'd expected either, and now she was getting ready to spend a holiday with a family she'd barely met.

"Sophie, I've got Amber checking some financial things about Eddie. Do you know if your mom gave him access to any of her banking or her investments?"

"No way."

"You're sure?"

"Pretty sure. She told me my dad worked hard for the money he left and if she invested it right we'd have enough. She was, like, *really* protective."

"That's good. So she didn't leave bank statements lying around the house or anything?"

"She didn't get that many, not that I ever saw."

"So she did her finances online."

"Right. I think so."

"She didn't share her passwords, did she? I guess what I'm getting at is whether Eddie could have got hold of the information so he could get into her accounts."

For the first time there was a pause. "I don't *think* so? I'm not sure. There was a little notebook in her dresser drawer where she wrote important things."

From being absolutely certain her mother's investments were secure, to sounding completely unsure ... now she had me feeling shaky about this.

"Sophie, one more thing. Think carefully. Can you remember the names of her banks or investment companies?"

"Oh sure. The stock broker place was called SR&O Investments. I remember that because we thought it was a lucky thing, those were my dad's initials. The bank, that's Desert Trust. The lady who worked there used to give me candy when I was little."

"Thanks, Sophie. This is helpful."

"Shall I keep trying my mom's phone? The battery's probably dead by now."

"Hey, we always stay hopeful, right? Maybe she's found a way to charge it back up."

"Right. Oh, here's Gracie again."

"Just one quick thing—two things. I heard Sophie mention Desert Trust. That's Sandy's bank, so if you need account information she can probably get it. Secondly, we're cooking a massive amount of food here, and we'd love to have you with us for Thanksgiving tomorrow. You know, if you haven't left by then. Sandy's coming and said she'd invite you, but I wanted to do it personally too."

I thanked her for the invite, although I still hoped to manage a way home. It was nice to know, anyway, that I had good people to spend time with if that's how it worked out. How would this have gone if I'd not met the Heist Ladies? After the dumpy motel in Holbrook, with Sophie in my care and the bad scene at Dixie's house, I could have ended up having a gloomy holiday.

I put all that aside and texted Amber the names of the bank and brokerage Sophie had shared. Then I called my dear husband to get an update.

"Yeah the cold front was fierce. Lots of wind," he said. "But you know Albuquerque. We got less than two inches of snow here. Looks like most of the storm energy was spent before it got to us."

"What are you hearing about the road conditions?"

"Mostly what's on the news. But our fuel truck came through early this morning. According to Joe out at the airport, the driver said the southern route is no problem at all. He came from Tucson, then north on I-25. Ran into rain and wind. No snow or ice."

That was good to know. Still, I needed to play it by ear. Was it worth dashing out of here and driving the extra hours on the longer route, just to eat turkey at home instead of at Gracie's? Then I glanced out Sandy's living room window. The Highlander sat in the driveway, a reminder that the southern route wasn't going to work for me. I had to return the SUV and pick up Ron's Mustang. That meant driving I-40.

"Text me an update if you hear anything new," I said. "Meanwhile, I'm deep into figuring out how to get this girl and her mother back together."

He laughed. "That's my Charlie. Right in the thick of things."

He was right. Why couldn't I get Sophie more involved in this? I called her again. "Remember I mentioned that Eddie had a son named Alex? He's around twenty, twenty-one … When you're finished helping Gracie with the dinner plans, could you prowl around whatever social sites a guy his age is likely to be on, see if you can find a picture to send me? I'm supposed to go looking for this guy and I have no idea what he looks like. Plus, I'd love to see if he's bragging about what he's up to."

"Yeah, okay. I can do that."

"We're looking for any kind of clues about where your mom might be. So really watch for anything that mentions her. Or his dad—see if he's talking about losing his father or anything like that. Remember, he goes by

Alex or Alexander and the last name could be Peppard or Planchard."

"I *get* it. I'll look."

And there she was again, snippy Sophie. I guess I completely overexplained the mission.

I stared out the window for several minutes, pondering my next move. When I heard my phone ping with a text, I dashed back to the kitchen to take a look.

It was from Amber: Vehicle plate you gave is registered to Valley Pawn. VP owned by Chaco Kaynor. Reputation of the biz is that they make shady loans. Hope this helps.

It did help. I'd felt fairly certain Kaynor owned Valley Pawn, but my guess that he was a loan shark seemed backed up now. Looked like we had a pretty good idea where Linda's money went. I thought of the tiny pawnshop in the unimpressive little business center. It hardly represented the image of an international money laundering operation. More like goons who paid visits in dark alleys and demanded pay-up-or-else from the clients.

So, how did Alex's moving Linda's money through offshore accounts relate to Eddie's debt (presumably) with this Kaynor dude?

I needed to see if I could catch up with Alex today, and I'd need to do it in a way that bypassed the doorman in that fancy building or the supposed housekeeper who served as gatekeepers. I paced back and forth a little, debating strategy.

My phone vibrated in my hand, startling me. The text this time was from Sophie.

Alex Planchard has accounts on TikTok, Insta, and Snap. Doesn't use his own photo. Avatar attached.

I stretched the tiny image larger to see details. It was

basically a cartoon image depicting a hip young man with a charming smile and a swoop of honey-blonde hair across his forehead. I wondered whether it even resembled the real guy. People generally created these to look somewhat like themselves—there were actually apps that would take your own photo and make up an image for you—but for a person operating outside the law, nothing would prevent him from making his social media avatar an exact opposite.

I thanked Sophie and decided to head out. Time was slipping by and I was no closer to locating Dixie than I'd been yesterday. I'd promised Rosalie I would find out what I could about Alex Peppard aka Planchard and I knew Amber would share the info she'd gathered, through Pen and Sandy. Knowing about his dirty tricks, I'd begun to wonder if the Eddie and Alex team had been targeting Dixie in a similar way, and it seemed the best way to get a feel for what was going on would be to confront Alex directly.

Amber could track the money; I needed to track the people.

I retraced my route to Scottsdale and found the upscale condos again without any problem. A different doorman and a female concierge were on duty this morning. She must have been newer at the job because she didn't give me the haughty look or bother to phone upstairs. I signed a register in an unreadable scrawl, and the name of the resident I was visiting. She glanced at the book and pointed me toward an elevator where the door slid open on its own. "It's programmed to take you to the fifth floor," she said.

How chichi.

The ride took all of four seconds, so I had little time to plan my intro. I decided to go with the truth, to offer condolences about his father and inform Alex of Linda's death.

The man who met me at the door appeared even younger than I'd imagined. I knew he was maybe a tad over twenty-one, although you could put a backpack on him and he could walk around a high school campus easily. A deep voice was the only contradiction to the young kid image.

At the moment he was dressed as a billionaire mogul, wearing a black t-shirt, black jeans, black running shoes. With the tousled blonde hair, blue eyes, and ready smile, his avatar wasn't actually that far off. He led me into a living room that some designer must have created for him. Everything but the couch was stark white. That piece was pure black. He didn't exactly offer me a seat but I took one anyway.

"So, how can I help you, Officer …?"

He thought I was a cop? Okay, I could go with that for now.

"We're looking into the death of Linda Ratcliff and some allegations made by her daughter."

His pretend-casual attitude tensed a little. "My stepmother died from cancer. What's to investigate? I thought you and Hernandez were trying to figure out who killed my dad."

There was a lot to unpack here. "Wait—stepmother?"

"Yes. Linda Ratcliff. She and my dad were together nearly five years."

Right. But they were never married. I let that slide. For now.

"Hernandez is looking into your father's murder. I'm doing some follow up."

"I told him everything I know about that."

"Right. What can you tell me about Dixie O'Connell? She was your dad's latest girlfriend, right? He'd been living in her house."

"I don't think so. Staying over, maybe. They partied. She was crazy about him, but it wasn't going anywhere serious."

"Have you heard anything from Dixie in the past week or so? Any idea where she is?"

A one-shoulder shrug. "Why would I?"

I couldn't tell if he was lying or not, but the quick glance toward the black jacket hanging over the back of a chair seemed like some sort of a tell.

"Back to Linda," I said. "He wasn't living with her anymore. I had that conversation with her personally before she died."

He gave me a steady gaze, revealing nothing. "What are you getting at?"

I met the stare. "Basically, money. Linda's accounts are missing a lot of it."

He put on a gentle smile. "Linda was such a generous woman, so caring, so giving. She wanted Dad and me to have a good life."

"You're saying she willingly gave most of her fortune to an unrelated man she'd known for only a few years? They were never legally married. Her daughter has been going through her records and—"

"That Rosalie is a liar and a bitch. She's the one who coerced her mother into cutting my dad out." He straightened and stood up. "I think you'd better speak to my lawyer."

I stood, as well. "We'd be happy to do that. Give me the contact information."

He held up an index finger and turned away. The moment he disappeared down a short hallway, I leapt on the black jacket, running my hands over it. A crinkling sound, fingers fished down into a pocket, and I came out with a receipt. Valley Pawn. Hm. It was stapled to a card but I didn't have time to look. I jammed both items into the side pocket of my purse a split second before Alex came back into the room.

"My attorney is with one of the top firms in the city." He handed over a business card with a little flourish.

I took it before he could realize that if I really were a cop, I'd be taking him downtown and that's where the lawyer would come into it. I pocketed the card and headed for the door. In a decent Columbo imitation, I stopped just before touching the handle.

"One other question. Chaco Kaynor."

His composure slipped, just a tad, and the smug smile disappeared. "What about him?"

"He and your father seemed to do a lot of *business.*"

Alex turned away and pretended to straighten a white vase on the white shelves beside the white fireplace. When he turned back toward me, his smooth calm was back. "I don't know the man."

Smug little creep.

"If you'll excuse me, I'm supposed to be at the funeral home in thirty minutes," he said, effectively pushing me out the door. "In the future, you cops should speak directly with my attorney."

"Wait—you said that earlier. What makes you think I'm a police officer?"

"You and Hernandez … he was here yesterday … So, you're not?"

I thought back. I'd been sitting in my car after a frustrated attempt to get upstairs to see Alex. Hernandez and I had exchanged a few words. Alex must have been observing. I had to wonder what else he'd been watching.

Chapter 34

I gravitated back over to the same Starbucks I'd visited yesterday. The wind had picked up, a chill reminder that, even this far south, a cold front had passed through. I parked, gathered my jacket tighter around me, and walked past a bougainvillea that didn't look too happy about the temperature drop.

Minutes later, with my latte in hand I drifted back out to my vehicle and made a call to Pen. She recognized Alex's lawyer's name.

"He's a shark," she said. "The kind who seems involved any time there's a high-profile case where he has the chance to get some shyster off the hook. Or to look good on camera—he's a very handsome man."

"I wonder why Alex thinks he needs a lawyer at this point. He accused Rosalie of being out to get him, basically.

Do you think that's why?"

"I'm having lunch with Benton today and I shall ask that question. Better yet, join us if you'd like."

I demurred for about four seconds. She convinced me that the food at a place called Mickey's was well worth it, and the atmosphere was casual. She gave directions and I agreed to meet them at 11:45. A vivid blue Tesla glided into the Starbucks parking lot, catching my eye. But what caught my eye even more was the driver. Alex Peppard.

He got out and sprinted inside, came back a couple minutes later with a grande cup in hand. He wore the same black Zuckerman-lookalike outfit, with the addition of the jacket that had been on the chair in his condo. Hmm. Maybe I could learn something if I followed along to see how his morning unfolded.

I can't say that I'm an expert at stealthy following, but I've had a little experience over the years. And the bright blue car was fairly easy to spot from a distance. Alex drove as though he were on the racetrack, zipping and dodging other cars and I worried a little about losing him at a traffic light.

But he soon got onto the ramp for the 101 Loop, heading south toward Paradise Valley (I sort of prided myself on knowing vaguely where that was). A few exits farther, the Tesla left the Loop and made a couple of quick moves, pulling into the lot of a huge funeral home.

Luckily, there must have sbeen a funeral in progress because the lot was full enough, I had no trouble keeping out of Alex's sight. I parked where I could watch his car as he got out and walked inside. If he was here for the funeral, I could be wasting an hour or more. But he'd told me he had an appointment. Surely that meant he was here to make the arrangements for Eddie's ultimate destination.

My wait was actually shorter than I'd dared dream. Alex came back out fifteen minutes later, hopped in his car and glided out the exit. I didn't quite glide, but I was right behind. Next move was north to Shea Boulevard and east to Fountain Hills, where we ended up—not surprisingly—at the Sculpted Rock Casino.

Alex drove up to the valet parking stand while I watched from twenty yards away. The young valet on duty glanced around and left. The man who came out through the massive glass front doors had a familiar size and shape. It was the huge goon who'd warned me away last night. I stared, half hoping Alex would get the same warning, but of course that was not to be. The big guy reached into his jacket and came out with an envelope. It might have been my imagination, but the parcel seemed stuffed with cash. Okay, yeah, there's no way I could actually *know* that.

Alex handed him something in return. A receipt? Yeah, right. But it could have been a drug packet or something like that. I reminded myself to stick to the facts, and other than witnessing some kind of transaction, I really knew nothing.

As Alex pulled away from the portico and I prepared to follow, I saw the goon look straight at my vehicle. Instinctively, I slid down to get out of sight. When I risked a peek, the big man was scanning the whole parking lot and Alex was already out the exit and into the traffic. Suddenly, I just wanted out.

By the time I got on the street again, Alex was nowhere in sight so I decided to give up on him. I wasn't quite sure what I'd learned, but there'd been some action this morning and I could either report it to the authorities or file it away in my little mental storage bank until I needed the information.

I pondered all this as I headed toward the lunch place where Pen had invited me to meet her friend Benton Case, former district attorney of Maricopa County. For some reason I'd expected a place named Mickey's to be one step up from McDonalds's, but of course with Pen this was not the case. I walked into a small but classy spot with a European flair and white tablecloths. She was right about the casual atmosphere, though. Jeans and sweaters were prevalent, with the trim, silver-haired man sitting next to Pen wearing the only business suit I spotted.

Benton rose from his chair to greet me by name. "Pen has told me all about you."

Hopefully not *all*, such as my role in letting Sophie break into the house when she found Eddie's body. I smiled and took the chair he pulled out for me. We spent a few minutes in chit-chat and looking over the menu. Benton said he always had the fish special because the chef's sauce was exquisite. He actually used the word exquisite.

Pen was debating between a salad and a soup. I went with the same salad she chose.

"I went by to see Alex Peppard this morning," I told them.

"Did he actually tell you anything?" Benton seemed curious.

"He says he has no idea where Dixie O'Connell is. And about Linda Ratcliff, he called her his stepmother and claimed she was wonderful and generous with his father and with him. That was after I brought up the subject of money."

Pen sputtered. "Stepmother! No. Linda never married

Edward. She never would have."

"Alex says otherwise and it sounds like he feels perfectly entitled to all of her money, now that his father is gone."

"What- what rubbish!" She looked toward Benton for support.

"I spoke with Detective Hernandez again this morning," he said. "He says Alex Peppard claimed his father's body."

I reached into my purse and handed him the card from Alex's attorney.

"Oh. This is one of the dirty players, for sure," he told us. "You've heard of ambulance chasers? This guy is an estate chaser. He has a reputation for upending estate plans, ripping up trust documents in open court, basically grandstanding. And his clients are the very epitome of the Edwards and Alexanders of this world."

"You mean he could actually have Linda's wishes overturned in favor of Alex?"

"Depends on how ironclad her will and trust documents are. Did she make any changes in recent months?"

I glanced toward Pen and we all went silent as the server delivered our plates and asked about refills for our water glasses.

"I honestly don't know," Pen said once the young man had moved away. "Rosalie is still going through everything to see what she can learn. She did find an amendment dated several years ago that gave Edward the right to continue to live in her house. But Rosalie says her mother thought better of it, realized what a mess that would become, and changed it back."

"Alex called Rosalie a couple of nasty names and says she coerced her mother. He argued with me that Linda married his father. Surely that can be disproven in court?"

Benton gave a sad shake of the head. "Each small point probably can be proven, such as the fact there was never a legal marriage. But, you never know what will happen in a courtroom. I've seen people just like Rosalie, with what seemed like ironclad cases, get overturned and have their lives upended by a greedy outsider like this Eddie. Judges and juries can make terrible mistakes when they fall for a con artist's story."

I picked at the cranberries in my salad and I noticed Pen hadn't touched hers.

"But there are appeals, aren't there? Ways to get someone to take a reasonable look at the whole picture?"

He swallowed the bite he'd been chewing. "Ideally—and this is what I'd advise your friend Rosalie—you don't want it to go to court. The process and the legal fees will eat her up."

"So … what? Pay this scumbag even *more* money to make him go away? That's extortion!" I caught the fact that the people at the next table had overheard, and I lowered my voice. "That's crazy! How can crooks get away with this?"

He dabbed his mouth with the cloth napkin in his lap, then placed his hand over mine. "Charlie, it happens every day. If only the lonely and lovesick people of this world could spot these shysters before they get involved. But they don't."

I thought of both Linda and Dixie, each widowed about a year before Eddie came into their lives. Had he watched obituaries, seeking out a vulnerable woman and setting up his plan? It wouldn't surprise me.

Pen sighed. "It's so sad, especially considering the amount of money these crooks have already taken from the accounts. Rosalie's had to freeze everything so they can't get more."

A smile crossed Benton's face and a dimple showed. "And I'll bet a certain team of ladies are working on this …?"

She didn't answer but the mood lightened a little. He was right. At least we were working on it. I discovered my salad actually tasted wonderful. When I was about halfway through my lunch, I decided to run some of the other names past Benton.

"In my search for Dixie O'Connell, I've run across several other people and I'm finding links between them. Let me know if you are familiar with any of these."

He gave a nod.

"Jorge Gadiz. Seems to be in some upper management position at Sculpted Rock Casino."

"Slick. He plays the hotshot, dresses the part, schmoozes the crowd at the casino, yes."

"Is he into anything illegal out there? Maybe laundering the money or loan sharking or something like that?"

He shook his head. "We never thought so. Jorge, being in an official position, knows the gaming authorities could cause a lot of trouble. Fine the casino or shut them down. Fine him personally or send him to jail if they could prove a strong enough case. We watched him for years, but he stays just short of getting his hands quite *that* dirty."

"There's a young woman named Carleen. Sorry, I didn't get her last name. Worked with Dixie as a volunteer at a dog rescue place. I saw her later the same day out at the casino, getting pretty cozy with Jorge. Maybe she's a girlfriend of his … maybe she was something of a go-between to facilitate the relationship with Dixie?"

"I'm not familiar with her name. I can ask around. If

she's actually with Jorge, she'd just be the latest in a long string of women. He's known for having lots."

"What about Dixie? I wonder if she might have been one of them. Apparently she loves to party."

"I'll ask. A golfing buddy is head of the gaming commission and they send agents around, undercover, to get a feel for activities that might bear watching more carefully. Informal surveillance. Eyes and ears, you know. If you have pictures of these women, I can put them out there."

I had a photo of Dixie I'd sneakily sent to myself from Sophie's phone. I described Carleen as best as I could. "Want me to try and get a picture of her?" Not that I wanted to take on another assignment right now.

He shook his head as he looked at Dixie's picture. "Send me this. You've said this Carleen frequents the place, and I'll mention that to the commissioner."

"Thanks. There's another name that came up. Chaco Kaynor, who is somehow connected with Val—"

"Valley Pawn. Law enforcement definitely know that one. He's been arrested and tried for illegal lending and using intimidation tactics to collect. Loansharking. He's got a couple of enforcers. One's a huge goon of a man known as El Asesino. The Assassin. His real name is Felipe Muñoz."

"I think Carleen was in a black Suburban with Chaco Kaynor last night. He let himself in the back door of Valley Pawn and said something to the woman in the car. I caught her name."

Both Benton and Pen looked a little sideways at me. "Please don't tell me you're lurking in dark alleys, following that man," he said.

Okay, I won't tell you that.

"Charlie, these are guys you don't want to cross. They don't mess around."

I covered my nervous gulp by drinking some of my water.

"I saw Alex Peppard this morning. He left his condo and drove out to Sculpted Rock, pulled up to the front door and exchanged something in an envelope with this Muñoz dude."

"Did either of them see you?"

"I'm pretty sure they didn't. I stayed in my vehicle, at a distance."

"Still, it's best if you don't go back out to the casino for a while. All of them—Jorge, Chaco, and Muñoz—have sharp eyes and excellent memories. They'll notice and they'll pay attention if they see you more than once."

"Good advice. I'll keep away." I noticed Pen was finished with her salad.

It was time to wind up the lunch visit and get back to whatever I would do next. I offered to split the check but Benton the gentleman insisted it was his treat. I left the two of them at Mickey's. As I got in the Highlander, I thought of them again. I liked the relationship Benton and Pen shared, and I wondered if they were lovers. At their age, maybe the passion had settled into a loving friendship. I adored that and hoped Drake and I would have the same camaraderie as we grew old together.

Chapter 35

I was halfway to Sandy's house before I'd fully formulated a plan for what to do next. My hostess wouldn't be off work for another hour or so, but that was fine. I could use some time on my own to ponder everything I'd learned. I let myself in and was immediately greeted by the cats.

"Oh no, you guys. I'm not putting out more food. Your mama knows when and how much to give you. Not me."

They continued to rub against my ankles as I walked into the kitchen and turned on the gas flame under the kettle. A cup of tea sounded good, and Sandy had picked up some pumpkin spice cookies at the bakery yesterday. I'd swear I remember her saying it was fine to help myself. So I did.

For some reason, I tend to think better on the move so I began to pace through the house. The cats quickly decided they couldn't be bothered with this restless new human in their midst, so they settled on the breakfast nook window seat and pretended not to watch me. I went through my list of suspects for the murder of Eddie Peppard.

Dixie seemed the most likely, no matter how much none of us wanted to see her accused and put on trial for it. He'd been found in her kitchen with her knife in him. The police couldn't ignore that, but I was looking at the deeper motives. Eddie owed money to some nasty guys.

So there were Jorge Gadiz and Chaco Kaynor and the loan enforcement team of Muñoz and whoever the other weasel was. But in a lot of ways it made no sense for them to kill the guy who owed them money. They were not the types who could get on the list of official debtors and stand in line for the courts to award them some money.

Alex Peppard, however, would be in line to inherit. In fact, he'd insinuated that he was somehow due Eddie's share of Linda's estate, and seemed ready to put his sleazy lawyer on the path to collecting it. I knew Rosalie would fight that to the bitter end, but meanwhile maybe Alex had taken matters into his own hands. Would he have actually killed his father so he could move up the line and get to Linda's money right away? Or did he see that as a lost cause, beyond what they'd already taken, and now have his sights on Dixie?

That seemed more likely. Alex was closer to Dixie's age, and I'd gotten the vibe that he found her fun and interesting. Maybe he'd tried to seduce her away from his father. Maybe she was willing. She always acted younger than her age, so a 21-year-old wasn't outside her cougary realm. Father and son both wanted the same woman … an argument escalated …

The kettle was screaming away in the kitchen and I

hurried from the living room to rescue it. With tea mug and a second cookie in hand, I settled at the breakfast table. Thinking of Dixie, I went back to her coworker, Carleen. Benton had discounted her, but I still felt she was somehow a player in the drama. I was still mulling that thought when the connecting door to the garage opened and Sandy walked in.

"I do love a short work week," she said, setting her briefcase on the floor near the door and shrugging out of her coat. "The bank is open Friday, but I don't have to be there. Yay!"

I smiled and told her the kettle was hot. I also admitted to taking two of the pumpkin cookies.

"I'm about to join you, the minute I'm out of these clothes and into my comfies."

She returned in under ten minutes, minus the skirt-suit and heels, snuggled into knit pants and a roomy fleece top. While she reheated the kettle, chose a teabag, and fussed over the cats' dinner, I gave the CliffsNotes version of my day so far: the visit to Alex's condo, following him, lunch with Pen and Benton.

"Busy day, you."

"No kidding. And I still don't have a clue where to find Dixie. Or even if she's the one who killed Eddie."

Sandy nodded, her mouth pursed as she considered. "A crime of retaliation, a crime of passion, or what?"

"Exactly. What, indeed?" I ran through my list of suspects with her, hoping she would see something I'd missed or that maybe my own thinking would settle on an answer by repeating.

"Well, in the retaliation-as-motive column could certainly go the men he owed money to," she suggested.

"I thought of that. Maybe there was a fight that got out of hand. Would they really want to kill their golden goose?"

"And why would Eddie still owe them, if he's managed to stash most of Linda's money in offshore accounts, as Amber suggested?"

"Right. That makes no sense. So, maybe the retaliation is coming from one of the women. Either Dixie or Linda could have motives there."

"Except, since Linda had nowhere near the strength to face down a man, at that point in her illness, it sort of throws suspicion back at Rosalie."

True. Linda's daughter had been on my radar earlier, but somehow I'd let that slip. Maybe I should put her back on the list.

"I was seriously looking at Alex, Eddie's son. He just has that look about him, the modern-kid entitlement. I get the feeling he has no scruples about cheating his way to the top. You see the types on the news all the time, everything from cheating on school assignments to forming corporations and raiding the assets for their personal fun, mansions, and jets."

"Are we seriously thinking he'd take cheating up a notch and include killing? Killing his own father?"

"It's been a thing ever since Oedipus."

"Hmm, true. Sex and money are two very powerful motivators." She'd carried her mug to the table and now enticed me with a third cookie.

I took one, even though I would probably regret it when I got back home to my bathroom scale. "I'd say Alex is more into the money. From what Amber told us, his moves seemed all about moving money in and out of a bunch of different accounts. As if tricking the police and banking authorities meant he was winning the game."

Some little thing clicked in my memory banks right about then. I walked into the living room where I'd dropped my purse on the sofa when I arrived. In the front zipper pocket was the receipt I'd nabbed from Alex's jacket pocket. I pulled it out and looked at it. As I remembered, the slip of paper was a receipt from Valley Pawn. Whatever Alex had bought there, it was noted simply by a stock number—NC38295—and had cost $300, plus tax. The receipt was signed by Chaco Kaynor.

"Whatcha got?" Sandy was now at the refrigerator, scouting out dinner ideas, perhaps.

I held up the receipt. "Stapled to the back is a business card for the pawnshop. No idea why Alex would need their card, since it seems he was already there."

"Something's written on the back," she pointed out.

I turned it over. A partial address was written at the top edge, with a series of scribbled lines below.

Sandy moved to stand beside me. "Looks like a map. Maybe directions to the address that's written there."

"Let's just check this out." I moved back to the table where I'd left my phone and entered the address: 15 Skull Canyon. "Skull Canyon? Really? I swear, you really have some picturesque place names here in Arizona."

She laughed. "For sure."

"Do you know where this is?"

"Not really. What does the map say?"

I stretched the map larger to see where the little red balloon had landed. The address was on a Skull Canyon Road. When I adjusted the size and moved the map back and forth, it look like Skull Canyon Road appeared to be a winding track that led out of a nearby town called Sunny Valley. The contradiction of images made me chuckle.

"Okay, Sandy, I'm still lost. Any idea where this Sunny Valley is?"

"North of the metro area, maybe an hour or so? I've never been there but I remember seeing exit signs for it off I-17. I think. You ought to verify that."

I did, and she was right. "Do you think this is a residence? A business?"

"Try Zillow?"

I went there and entered the information, but there was no listing. It seemed the place was too far out for the real estate market to care much about it. There was one listing in all of Sunny Valley, and I wouldn't describe it as a charming little place. It, and the surrounding neighborhood, seemed beyond fixer-upper; it was definitely rundown.

"Alex wouldn't have had this map unless there was some reason important enough for him to go out there. And the connection with Chaco Kaynor and Valley Pawn is undeniable. What do you say?"

"Do I agree with that statement? Yeah. Seems obvious. Do I have a clue about the important reason? Sorry."

But all at once, I did have a clue. All the clues that had been collecting for days now.

"I have to go there," I told Sandy. "Now."

"No no, no-no-no." She placed a hand on my arm, as if that would stop me. "You're not heading out there. At least not on your own."

I told her what I'd overheard between Chaco and Carleen as I hid behind the dumpster last night. "It just hit me. I think they had Dixie, drugged, in the back seat of his Suburban. Alex would only have the map if he planned to join them. They're probably threatening her, or Sophie, so she'll give up her passwords."

I turned to look deeply into her eyes. "You don't have to come, Sandy. Finding Dixie is my mission."

"Hey, the Heist Ladies are in this with you now. Let's gather some help."

Chapter 36

Mary was in. No questions asked. Sandy had told me about her background—how she was homeless after her ex took everything, how she'd fought to get it back and became a martial arts expert as she took on a new business venture. Now, she arrived at Sandy's house, ready to kick some butt.

Gracie arrived ten minutes later, a little breathless. "All set," she told us. "The kids were curious, but Scott has all three of them content to watch TV. They actually agreed on which movie that would be."

She looked around. "Is Pen coming?"

"We decided not. There could be a confrontation," I told her. "I was a little worried about her safety, at her age."

"Don't let that fool you," Sandy said. "Pen's super sharp."

"But, yeah, I agree with Charlie," Mary added. "We don't know what we'll run into out there."

There was a little debate over the vehicles to take. One or two? SUV, minivan, or sedan? In the end, the Highlander seemed most suitable with its four-wheel-drive and the third row of seats, given the fact that we had no idea what we would encounter. The mission was to come home with Dixie in our custody but we had no idea whether that was possible. I felt doubts creep in as we stopped to gas up. What was I doing here?

* * *

It was a little after nine p.m. when we exited I-17 for Sunny Valley and wound our way through low hills for ten or twelve miles before we came to any signs of life. Pretty much as our Zillow search had showed, there wasn't much left of the town, which Mary informed us had been some kind of military outpost in the 1800s, and never did take off as a retirement mecca the way so many other places in Arizona had.

The two-lane paved highway formed the main street and boasted a concrete block gas station/convenience store with peeling paint and a faded sign. It appeared to have been closed down years ago. Margie's Café was similarly shuttered, and Jake's Liquor Store looked iffy, at best. At ten-thirty p.m. we spotted only a couple of lights in houses, which sat back on the town's one cross street. The residences were an odd mix of Depression-era bungalows and what appeared to be a 1980s attempt to revitalize with more upscale structures.

"Hard to tell how many of these places are actually

occupied," Gracie commented.

My guess—not many. "Sandy, consult our little map and let me know where I should turn."

We'd brought flashlights, and she pulled hers out and aimed it at the back of the Valley Pawn business card. "It shows that intersection we just passed, so it looks like the next right-hand turn will be it. Then the road does some wiggles and he's put an X on the left."

The so-called wiggly part of the dirt road had a number of side roads carved out, in both directions, and I tried the first two only to find myself on tracks that petered out right away. I backed out of each and tried again. A broken and faded real estate sign indicated this might once have been an attempt at a subdivision.

"Ladies, what do you think?"

"I spotted a light," Mary said. "Maybe another quarter mile ahead."

I realized it was so dark and so quiet out here that everyone in town had probably heard our vehicle pass through or spotted our lights.

Of course, if Chaco Kaynor's place had any kind of security in place—a high lookout spot, sentry guards, or dogs—we were toast already.

Two more bends in the road and I spotted the light Mary had noticed. I cut the Highlander's headlights and let the SUV roll along as quietly as possible until we came to what must be the driveway, on the left. I cruised past and we all stared at the collection of structures.

A house sat at the end of the long drive. A vehicle was parked in front of it, but it wasn't the black Suburban I'd seen before. Was Chaco here, or did the plain sedan belong to a bodyguard? Or did we actually have the right house? The good news came from the bluish light at a large, uncurtained window. The TV was on, and hopefully had masked our approach.

I drove past the place, turned around, and positioned our ride a little beyond the driveway, in what I hoped was the best getaway position possible.

"I'll go scout it out," Mary offered.

"You haven't seen Chaco. Maybe I'd better do it. I'll be right back." I left the key in the ignition and shut my door quietly.

Aiming my small flashlight directly at the ground helped me avoid the ruts and toe-breaker rocks along the drive, as I made my way toward the two-story Spanish mission style house. On the left of it was an attached garage with two bays. On the right, stood a separate casita with dark windows. Two other small buildings sat behind that. I didn't risk flashing my light toward them; I guessed them to be garden sheds or small workshops. The property had a dozen or more tall trees, desert varieties, and an attempt had been made to landscape around the house with bougainvillea, bird of paradise, and a variety of cactus.

I glanced toward the large garage, wondering if there were additional vehicles inside. The only way to know how many people were on site was to check it out. I avoided stepping into the pool of light from the front window, doused my flashlight and used ambient light to make my way around the thorny plants so I could peer inside.

A television screen the size of a royal banquet table was mounted on the wall to my right, and a man was sprawled on the sectional sofa across from it, sucking down a Corona Light to go with his football game. It wasn't Chaco.

I scanned the rest of the great room and didn't see

anyone else, but there was light from another space to the left. A glimpse of countertop told me that would be the kitchen. I backed away and circled the house, toward the second light. The kitchen was sleek and modern and a total mess. Dirty dishes stood in haphazard stacks on the counter, beer bottles covered half the center island, and a very greasy looking skillet sat on a stove burner. An overflowing trash bin at the end of the island spewed take-out containers, and two pizza boxes lay nearby. I guessed that it took more than just the one guy in the living room to create all this clutter.

A step back gave me a view of the rear of the home. Besides the kitchen and living area, there were two smaller windows I judged to be bathroom or utility room sized. A long blank wall could be the back of the garage. Upstairs, a row of four windows probably indicated bedrooms and baths.

A sliding glass door to the left led to the great room, showing me a long dining table that sat between me and the big space where the guy was still there in front of the television. A smaller, walk-through door stood to the right.

"What are you doing?" came a whisper in my left ear. Mary stood there.

I slapped a hand over my mouth to suppress my shriek. My leg bumped something and sharp cactus spines went right through my jeans. "What are *you* doing here?"

"We all got worried. You've been out here almost fifteen minutes and we were afraid they'd caught you."

"Did Sandy and Gracie come too?" I asked, gingerly touching the denim to see whether the cactus had left its thorns with me.

"No. I told them to give me a few minutes to find you,

and if neither of us came back they should go for help."

"Okay, go back and tell them I'm fine." I gave the quick recap of what I'd seen and the layout of the house as much as I could gather. I pulled her away from the view of the windows, making my way toward the walk-through door that I hoped would lead to the garage or show me a way to get upstairs.

"Do we even know we have the right place?"

"I'm going inside to see what I can learn. I'll text you. If I don't find any evidence to connect the place with Dixie or Eddie, I'll get out and we'll try something else." I turned the doorknob and it opened.

Mary didn't seem overly pleased with that plan, but someone needed to go back and reassure the others or we'd lose our ride back. She walked away, not even bothering with her flashlight. The woman must have the night vision of a cat.

I stepped inside and gave my eyes a minute to adapt to the dark. I was in a short hallway, almost a vestibule, with some cabinets on one side, a doorway to a laundry room ahead of me, and another door. By the grimy handprints on it, I guessed this went to the garage. I opened it and peeked out with my handy flashlight. Yep, garage. Both bays were empty. The one nearest me had tracks on the concrete floor and that empty-space feel that meant something was normally parked there. The other bay held a couple of large toolboxes, the red ones professional mechanics use, and a mountain bike with one flat tire.

I backed away and took a long, slow breath. So far, nothing I'd seen was connected with my reasons for being here.

A shuffling sound around the corner raised my

heartbeat a notch. I realized I was only five or six feet from the kitchen, and someone was in there. I stepped into the laundry room and flattened myself against the wall.

The fridge opened, bottles rattled, it closed again. A beer run for Mr. TV. The footsteps came toward me and I held my breath, but they veered in another direction. There must be a bathroom nearby because in a moment I heard the distinctive sound of a male aiming a stream into a toilet. Of course. That's what went along with emptying a beer and starting another. I remained quiet until he'd finished, burped loudly, and picked up his new beer. Then a phone rang.

Must be the guy's cell because he answered with, "Yeah?" Two seconds of silence, then, "All quiet here. Stuff you put in the water really works." Another two seconds. "'Kay. See you then."

Whatever that meant. At least the unknown man had shuffled back toward the television and I could breathe again. I hovered at the edge of the kitchen until I could see him across the room and be assured he was absorbed in the game. I spotted a flight of stairs leading upward. But did I dare cross behind the man and try for them? Only an open shelving unit divided the spaces.

Again, I wondered … what if we had the wrong place or I'd somehow misread the whole situation?

Then I looked down. At the base of the kitchen island lay a pair of women's red cowboy boots. Exactly like Sophie's.

Chapter 37

A buzzing started in my ears. Dixie was here. Without giving myself time to think about it or chicken out, I slipped past the shelves and headed for the stairs. Thank goodness they were carpeted. I peered from the landing down to the living room and saw the guy was still absorbed.

A long hall stretched in front of me, with doors leading off both sides of it. The first led to a bathroom, where I ducked in long enough to send a fast text to Mary.

I'm upstairs. Dixie's here somewhere. One guard as far as I can tell. I'll find her and figure out how to meet you guys.

In response: I'm coming too.

Don't come inside. Just watch the man. Let me know if he heads upstairs.

A thumbs-up emoji.

I jammed the phone into my back pocket and began

to systematically check the rooms. Some of the doors stood open, so I gave them only a quick glance. A master bedroom with ensuite bath, another bedroom with two bunkbeds, a small study. That one interested me enough to go in and check it out.

A rolltop desk sat against a wall with tall windows on both sides of it. The small drawers were too many to go through, but the cardboard box full of bundled cash looked interesting. I pulled out my phone again and snapped a picture of it. The flash went off. Shit! I'd better be careful.

No sound other than the game on TV came from downstairs and I took a careful peek into the hall before exiting the study. The last door at the end of the corridor was closed. That had to be my target. I headed straight for it and gingerly tested the knob. Locked.

That never stopped me. As a kid I'd developed tricks for breaking into my brothers' bedrooms to get into their stuff and gather blackmail material for favors in exchange for my silence with the parents. I'm an old hand at this. Except that I'd left my purse in the Highlander and I wasn't at home where I had a supply of paperclips and bobby pins and other gadgetry. I stood there a second, thinking.

The rolltop. It was like an office supply store at my fingertips. I went back there and located the perfect thing, a business card that had been laminated to just the right thickness. Back at the locked door, it slid between the knob and the strike plate, and voila. An open door.

I shone my flashlight inside, making certain I hadn't just opened a pit of vipers or cage of lions or something. But no. The sparsely furnished room held a single bed with a lone woman who groggily raised her head when the light hit her face.

"Dixie? Dixie O'Connell?" I whispered, slipping into

the room and closing the door behind me. I switched on a small lamp on a nightstand.

She rolled over and pulled the puffy comforter more tightly around her shoulders.

I recognized her from the pictures on Sophie's camera, although she was dirty and disheveled, and there was no ready smile this time. I shook her shoulder. "Dixie! I'm here to help, to get you out of here. You need to wake up!"

Her eyes focused on me finally, a little. "What—?"

"Dixie, I've been with Sophie. I brought her home to you but we couldn't find you."

Her head nodded but she really seemed out of it.

"Pay attention. I need you to focus, Dixie. I need to get you out of this house and back to Sophie."

"Sophie? She's here?"

"Almost. I can take you to her."

"Water ... so thirsty." She reached for a glass on the nightstand and I grabbed it away from her. On the floor beside the stand were several plastic jugs with more.

"No, not yet. You've been drugged, using the water. We'll get you some that's better. But you have to come with me. Can you sit up?" I got an arm around her shoulders until she was sitting in the middle of the bed.

She gripped her head with both hands. "Headache. Awful."

"I'm sure. I don't know what they've given you, but we can get you to a doctor once we're out of this house."

Exactly how I would manage that, I had no idea. Was the guard armed? Who had been on the phone with him, and were they on the way? I propped Dixie up and got a text out to Mary.

Found Dixie. Upstairs last bedroom at end of hall. Can you knock out the guard and get here to help?

Sure.

Semi-kidding about knocking him out. **Go carefully.**

Okay, now if I could just get Dixie on her feet and Mary could lure the guard out of the way, we might be able to stumble to my car and beat it out of here. I turned back to the moaning woman on the bed.

"Okay, Dixie, let's take this a step at a time. My name's Charlie. I need for you to stand up if you can."

"Carleen."

"No, it's Charlie. Charlie Parker."

But she was focused on something behind me. I spun around to find Chaco Kaynor standing in the doorway. And right behind him was Carleen, who I suspected was no longer going to be on Dixie's friend list.

"Charlie Parker. We meet at last," he said, giving me an oily smile.

Benton's words came back to me. I was facing down one very nasty character, and his henchman was now pushing his way into the bedroom. Dixie started to sob hysterically.

Chapter 38

My phone and flashlight were gone, and the space where they shoved us was black as pitch. When the hulking guard stormed the room and physically lifted Dixie from the bed, and then Chaco pulled a gun on me, well, there weren't many options but to go along. All I knew was that we were in the smallest of the outbuildings, in the middle of Godforsaken County, and the door had just slammed shut and a padlock clicked on the other side.

The place must have been a potting shed at one time. It smelled of garden chemicals like fertilizer. The floor was either very gritty or made of dirt. I wondered if they'd left any shovels behind—maybe we could dig our way out.

"Dixie? You okay?"

"Yeah, I'm here." Her voice came through much more clearly than earlier. I hoped she was coming out of the effects of the drug. She'd been pulled from the bed, barefoot and wearing dirt-crusted jeans and a plaid shirt.

"Charlie?" It was a new voice, one I knew. A cell phone flashlight light came on.

"Mary!" Joy and despair flooded me. "They caught you too."

"Yeah, dammit. I did a ninja move on that guard so I could get upstairs to help you, but the jerk knew the countermove. He whirled and whacked me in the head. Then Chaco and Carleen showed up. Once Chaco pulled the gun, I wasn't arguing anymore."

She was sitting with her back to one wall, her knees bent, one hand massaging her temple. She looked around. "I could use some water."

"Me too," Dixie said.

Carleen had carried three bottles of drinking water as the men hustled us outside. Now I knew why, when I saw them sitting on a shelf.

"No—don't drink it!" I explained how I knew the water had been drugged.

Dixie got an almost desperate look on her face.

"Sorry. There has to be something addictive in there, something that makes you keep wanting it, so we've got to get rid of it." I took the bottles and poured them out on the ground before she could stop me.

I considered our situation. Our team was down to a banker and a housewife. "What about Gracie and Sandy?"

Mary shook her head. "I don't know. I left them in the SUV and told them to stay there until they heard from us."

"How'd you keep your phone? Chaco took mine."

She tugged at the waist of her jeans, showing she had a pair of yoga pants on beneath them. "I felt cold all day. Guess that was good—I had my phone tucked into the inner waistband."

"Excellent. Tell Gracie and Sandy to get out of the area and then call for help."

"Got it." She picked up the phone, swiping at the screen to enter a number. The light began to flicker and dim, and then it went dead.

We were plunged into darkness again. I'd had time to take note of what was in the shed with us. No shovels, no picks or axes, not a tool of any kind. There was a narrow horizontal window high on one wall, but I'd already assessed it. Even if we'd had something to break it with, I couldn't see any of us—not even Mary with the narrow hips and firm body—being able to squeeze through.

"We'll wait it out," Mary said. "People know where we are."

I hoped so. Prayed that Chaco had not caught Sandy and Gracie, or we were pretty much cooked.

"While your phone was lit, did you happen to notice what time it was?" It's a quirk of mine, always wanting to know.

"Yeah. A little after midnight."

I glanced up at the skinny window, where I could barely see a few stars in the night sky. Morning sky. *It's Thanksgiving Day, and I'm as far from home as ever.* My mood plummeted again.

Chapter 39

Time passed. I dozed a little and weird dreams filled my head, images of storm troopers and running men and the flashes and booms of a war zone. Cold seeped into me from the ground. Someone moaned. I roused enough to remember where I was.

Mary was dreaming too, muttering in her sleep. Dixie was the one who'd moaned. I blinked and rubbed my eyes, realizing I could see a little. Flashes of light were visible at the high window. The images of my dreams became real.

"Wake up!" I reached out and jostled the others. "Something's going on outside."

Mary came to her feet almost instantly.

"Look—lights." I pointed at the window.

"Those are red and blue," Mary said. "Law enforcement?"

I had a vision of cops taking Chaco, Carleen, and the guard away into the night and the three of us being left here until we mummified. "Make noise! We have to let someone know we're in here." I began kicking at the door, pounding with my fists.

Dixie let out an ear-shattering scream.

"Yow, that's painful," Mary said, covering her ears. But she joined in with shouts of her own.

I kicked and pounded the door until my hands throbbed. Eventually I heard a voice.

"Hey, someone's in this shed."

"Yes! We're in here—let us out!" We all joined in.

A bright light shone around the edges of the door, and I heard scraping sounds—a pry bar or bolt cutter? I didn't care. Somebody was working on getting the door open and it didn't sound like Chaco's bunch.

When a chubby guy in a state trooper uniform finally yanked the door outward, I was never so happy to see anyone in my life. He seemed too confused to ask who we were, and we were too exhausted to explain.

I had only one question. "Two of our friends were here, waiting at the road in a green Highlander. Are they okay?"

He looked around for the answers. "I'm not sure."

He didn't need to invite us out of the shed; we all poured through the doorway. The dark night was now lit by a dozen or more vehicles, eerily reminiscent of the sight I'd witnessed during that odd night at the Sundowner Motel in Holbrook. But I didn't have time to think about that. I needed to know that Gracie and Sandy hadn't been captured, stuck into one of the other buildings on the property.

"Who's in charge here?" I asked the officer who'd let us out.

He glanced around and pointed toward a woman in a pantsuit and overcoat. I ran toward her, panting as I blurted out my question about our friends' safety.

"I'm FBI Special Agent Darla McGee. And you are?"

"Charlie Parker, from Albuquerque. I'm here to—" I realized the whole explanation would take way too long. "I just need to know that Chaco and his gang didn't harm Gracie and Sandy. They were sitting in a green Toyota out on the road in front of this house."

"There was no vehicle in front of the house when we arrived. We've been gathering evidence against Chaco Kaynor for months now, and we got a call from a Detective Hernandez in Mesa, about two hours ago."

It seemed logical to me that the only way Hernandez knew to send all these other agencies out here must have been because he heard it from our Heist Ladies team. I had to be content to wait before I'd know for sure. I thanked McGee, and then someone else stepped up and tapped her shoulder for attention.

I looked around and spotted Mary and Dixie, talking to a man I hadn't thought I'd ever care to see again. Hernandez. Dixie was limping on the rough gravel in the yard, and I asked someone to get her boots from the house. "Near the kitchen cabinets," I told them.

Hernandez herded us all into a vehicle in the driveway, where he confirmed what I'd hoped to hear about Gracie and Sandy. They'd been questioned and released to go home. He took statements from the rest of us, and told us Chaco Kaynor had been on the radar of the FBI and IRS for criminal usury—or loansharking—for months. There was a hint of professional smugness as he took credit for phoning the tip to them.

"You'll need a ride," he said. "Where to?"

I wasn't sure. I wanted to verify where Sophie was. Mary's phone was dead and mine was missing. "Did anyone take a phone from Chaco, one with a cover showing a photo of a cute brown and white spaniel?"

Hernandez actually smiled. "Like this one? Somehow, I didn't think this cover was Chaco's taste, and Carleen swore it wasn't hers."

I had enough battery left for one call and I made it a quick one.

"Gracie Nelson's house," I told Hernandez. "We're all gathering there."

"Sit tight in the car. I need to do one more thing here and then I'll give you a ride." He got out and left the heater running for us.

My little inner devil was tempted to slide behind the wheel and take off, to get back to the big city and wind things up without delay, but that would cause a great big drama and, truthfully, I didn't have a whole lot more fight left in me. It was a little after three a.m., according to the dashboard clock. I slid down in my seat and closed my eyes.

Chapter 40

I awoke when the squad car came to a halt at the curb in front of Gracie's house. The Highlander sat in the driveway, a nice reassurance that my friends had made it home safely. Well, that and the fact that the rental had come back unscathed. The house was dark except for the porch light and one downstairs room.

Mary got out of the back seat and told Dixie where we were. I turned to Hernandez.

"What about Alex Peppard? Was he involved in all this too?"

"That's a whole separate case. Edward Peppard was merely the link between them." He didn't seem inclined to say more.

I got out and wished Hernandez good luck, betting I would learn more from the Heist Ladies than the cops would ever share with me. The three of us walked up to Gracie's front door. We were debating whether to ring or knock when the door flew open; Sandy and Gracie came bursting out. They grabbed Mary and me in huge hugs, with a lot of laughter and a few tears.

Gracie let go of me and turned to our companion. "Dixie. It's so good to meet you, finally. There's a girl upstairs who's going to be absolutely thrilled that you're here."

We all tiptoed inside and up the stairs, where Gracie led us to the guestroom where Sophie had been staying. She eased the door open and pointed to the sleeping form on the bed. The room was softly illuminated by a nightlight in the adjoining bathroom. Dixie pulled off her red boots and slipped onto the bed beside her daughter. I swore I saw a single tear trickle down her cheek.

"Let's figure out what the rest of us are doing," Gracie whispered, drawing the door closed and heading for the stairs.

"Ohmygosh, Amber's still on the video chat," Sandy said, as we entered the kitchen. She walked over to the tablet that was propped against a cookie jar. "Hey, you still there? Guess who just showed up?"

Mary and I got into the picture to say hello. I flinched a little at my appearance, smoothing my messy hair and rubbing my hands over my face to bring a little color back to the wan complexion staring back at me. Mary wiped at a dirt smudge on her own face.

"You found Sophie's mother?"

"We did. They're snuggled together right now."

Gracie offered coffee or a couch and blanket, our choice. I opted for the coffee. My hit-and-miss sleep over the past few hours had, surprisingly, revived me.

"So what happened? Sandy and Gracie told me where you found Dixie. Was she there all this time?" Amber asked.

"I don't think so. Remember the night I had you trace the plate on the big dark SUV?" I filled everyone in on the snippet of conversation I'd caught between Chaco and Carleen. "I'm pretty sure Dixie was in the back seat, drugged into oblivion, and that's probably when they moved her from wherever she'd been, out to the place in nowheresville."

Amber nodded. "I found something that made me think they were trying to snatch Sophie from you. Not sure about the reason—maybe to use her as leverage to get Dixie to do what they wanted."

I'm sure my expression revealed my curiosity.

"It involves Alex Peppard. You told me someone woke you up by pounding on your motel door?"

"Yes, the night we stayed in Holbrook."

"Pretty sure that was Alex. Because of the timeframe, we'd pretty well ruled out either Eddie or Chaco."

"Right. But Alex? How on earth did he even know I existed? Or that Sophie was with me, in some random place off the interstate?"

"Dixie had received a call from Social Services, telling her you'd be bringing Sophie home. Maybe she shared that with Eddie, maybe they later intimidated her until she told … not sure. But he had your name and knew your general route. I found trackers online, where he'd searched your credit card records and learned the motel where you were staying."

"Wow." I felt the blood drain from my face. "Scary how much a person can find out."

"Well, not just *anyone*. I told you this guy has awesome hacking skills."

"So, has Alex been arrested in conjunction with the rest of this?" I asked the question to the group in general.

No one knew for sure. I remembered Hernandez's comment that Eddie's theft of money from the accounts of the women in his life was a separate case from the loansharking racket run by Chaco and his henchmen. And how did Carleen, Dixie's supposed friend and the lover of dogs, fit in? I realized there were still a bunch of unanswered questions. My crazy week from hell wasn't over yet.

Chapter 41

Sandy suggested that she and I go back to her place to clean up. "We can be back in plenty of time to help get the big dinner on the table," she said.

Questions and other thoughts were swirling through my head, but a hot shower and clean clothes would take precedence over everything else at this point. Daylight was barely a suggestion on the horizon as we walked into Sandy's house and headed for our own rooms.

I shed the clothing that had seen me through half a night on a dirt floor. I spent a good long time in the shower, letting the hot water soothe the aches from my limbs. Choosing a soft red sweater and clean jeans, I packed everything else. My mission was accomplished, although there were some goodbyes to be said.

And although Thanksgiving dinner wasn't happening

for hours yet, the Heist Ladies couldn't seem to stay apart as the latest case wound down. Albuquerque beckoned, but I couldn't resist being here in person to get the last of the details. We still didn't know who had killed Eddie Peppard.

We were back at Gracie's by mid-morning with mimosas and handheld mini-waffles for a light brunch. Amber was still on video at her spot on the tablet. So cute. Rosalie came, along with Pen and Mary. Dixie and Sophie were freshly showered and couldn't stay apart. I was thrilled to see that Sophie's reason for running away apparently had not been her relationship with her mom. The two were clearly very close.

"Hey, Sophie!" Gracie's daughter shouted from the far side of the great room. "You gotta see the Rockettes. They're in the parade."

Sophie rushed away to catch their performance on TV.

"She's in the phase right now where she wants to be a Rockette when she grows up," Dixie said. "Next month, who knows?"

"So, Dixie," I said, lowering my voice so the kids wouldn't hear. "What happened? Where were you all that time?"

She sank onto one of the barstools at the counter. "I went home early from the dog rescue. That was Thursday. I knew you'd be there with Sophie soon and I wanted to get the house ready. But the minute I walked in I knew something was going on. Eddie was in the kitchen, and there was a shouting match going on. Some argument about money and this other guy demanding more. I turned the corner and was about to tell them to take it outside. I wouldn't have that kind of fighting in my home." She took a sip of her mimosa.

"This big guy—Chaco—shoved Eddie and he fell. Hit his head on the edge of the counter, and he was staggering around, trying to stand up again. Furious. He pulled a knife out of the block, a big kitchen knife, but the other guy got it away from him and … I don't know how exactly. He rushed Eddie and the next thing I knew the knife was in his chest and he was down on the floor. I guess I screamed or something …"

"Oh my gosh, Dixie," Amber said, looking shocked.

"Chaco spun around and grabbed me, and I was so scared he'd kill me next. He dragged me out to a big black truck-thing and some other guy was waiting in there. At first he said he wouldn't hurt me if I'd just give him the money for Eddie's debts. What debts, I asked. I didn't know Eddie'd borrowed from guys like that."

"We went out to the casino, and I thought oh, okay. Jorge will explain things. I knew the casino crowd. Carleen and I used to hang out there some. But in the middle of the afternoon it was different. No band, no partying. Just all these mean-looking guys and all they said to me was they wanted money. If there's one thing I'm super responsible about, it's making sure Rob's money was kept safe for Sophie's education and our future. I wasn't about to pay off Eddie's gambling debts with it."

"How'd you end up out at that place so far away?" Mary asked. "And drugged? We could barely get you to wake up."

"It's really fuzzy. I guess they spiked my drink. Once in a while I'd wake up a little and I was in a hotel room … I think at the casino. But then later I was in a dark bedroom somewhere. No idea where or how I got there."

Rosalie had been quiet, but now she had a question.

"How did you and Eddie get together? I don't know if you know any of the history, but he'd been living with my mother, pretending they were married while he systematically cleaned out her life savings. It sounds like that's what he was after with you?"

"I think so. At first it was all about having a good time, just hanging out, drinking and dancing, gambling a little at the casino but not much. Carleen first took me there 'cause she liked Jorge a lot. You know, working together, she knew I'd lost my husband and was just looking for some fun. She knew I wasn't hurting for money, although I don't think I ever told her how well set Sophie and I were. Maybe she said something? That'd be my guess."

"So that would have been sometime last summer?" Rosalie asked. "That's when he started spending less time with Mother. She thought it was because she got sick. Once he knew she was dying he had no further interest ... something like that."

"Sounds like he simply found greener pastures," I suggested.

"And don't forget the money movements we discovered," Amber added.

"I heard from Carleen this morning," Dixie said. "She's really upset and super sorry that she got me involved with Eddie. She admitted she faked being me on the phone with Sophie. Jorge apparently ordered her to do it. She *says* she's ready to turn her life around, but I doubt I'll ever trust her again. Too bad. It was a fun friendship while it lasted."

Dixie glanced toward the other room, where teen laughter was prevalent. "I've got more important things in my life now, anyway."

Rosalie set her plate down, hard enough to catch our

attention. "Well, that Edward Peppard—that man was evil. I'm glad he's dead."

We all turned, a little shocked.

"He can't do this to another woman, ever again."

"I'm glad too," Dixie said simply. "I won't miss him at all."

Sadly, none of us would. I wondered how Alex felt about his father's death. I hadn't detected a whole lot of sorrow from him either.

"There is some good news," Amber said. "You all know I've been working on tracing Linda's money, to find out where Eddie and Alex stashed it. With all these law enforcement departments climbing over Eddie's business, we couldn't take the chance they'd freeze those accounts and make you wait years to get your money back."

"And ...?"

"It's coming—has already come—right back into Linda's accounts. Rosalie, you now have access again to your parents' savings."

Rosalie went pale for a moment, then her eyes filled with tears. Pen, Gracie, Mary, and Sandy smiled, not at all surprised at this revelation.

"Oh, and I may have phoned in a little anonymous tip to let them know Alex was the one orchestrating the thefts in the first place."

I had no idea how she could keep her own electronic fingerprints out of their sight, but that was apparently Amber's superpower. One more question lurked in my head, maybe related, maybe not.

"Back to that night Sophie and I were in Holbrook, I woke up to a bunch of flashing lights. Law enforcement seemed to be out in force, several different departments, even a fire truck or two. They were totally silent, and left after a few minutes. I never did figure out what that was all about."

Mary looked up sharply. "That was the same night you were there? I read something on the news ..." She pulled out her phone and brought up a page from her browser, reading aloud. "FBI and IRS agents enlisted help from various local Arizona law enforcement agencies as they staged a raid on a small roadside motel in Holbrook. The targets were two males suspected in multiple financial crimes. Other than stating that the man was not located on the property, the agent in charge declined to comment on the crimes, their victims, or the source of the tip that led them to the small town in northeastern Arizona."

Eddie? Chaco? Alex? It could have been any or all of them.

My phone rang, showing an unknown number. I stepped out of the crowd to take the call.

"Happy Thanksgiving, Charlie! It's Harvey. Harvey Molson. Are you back in Albuquerque?"

The old man's memory was still quite sharp on some subjects, I decided.

"Not quite. Working on it, though."

"Jeannie and I are having a nice Thanksgiving dinner here. She's been feeling better, and we'll go down to the dining room in an hour or so."

"Did you ever get your car back?"

"I'm afraid not. The police had no luck, but the insurance company paid for it. It was also suggested to me that maybe I'm at that point in life when I should give up driving. So I suppose I'll be taking the community van to run my errands from now on."

"Sounds easier, for sure."

"How's young Sophie doing? She was giving you some fits last week."

I glanced through the doorway into the family room, where the teens were busily thumbing away on their phones. Sophie had her red boots on again. "Things are a whole lot better now."

I wished him well and we said goodbye. It was time for me to do the same.

Chapter 42

With a call home to Drake and assurances that the highways had been sufficiently cleared, I bade an emotional farewell to the Heist Ladies. With each hug and invitation to return, I knew I'd made five new friends—friends for life. Make that seven. Dixie and Sophie were over the top in their appreciation, something I rarely receive from our regular clients at RJP. There were more than a few moist eyes as I walked out the front door and got in the Highlander, waving goodbye to the group huddled at Gracie's front door.

I sailed along on this leg of the road trip, much easier than the first time through. Traffic was almost non-existent as people gathered with family and friends instead of battling it out in their cars. I hit the outskirts of Holbrook in under three hours and, thanks to calling ahead, was able to switch my trusty rented Toyota for Ron's Mustang in just a few minutes time. Someone had freshly washed and detailed it and kept it stored in the garage during the week I'd been away. I slipped a generous tip to Casey, asking her to be sure the right person received it.

On Interstate 40 once again, the miles flew by and I savored the silence, although the past week had given me a renewed appreciation for camaraderie and those close to me. I thought of Linda and Rosalie, the loss and trauma for that little family. As for Dixie and Sophie, I hoped the teen would settle in and be happy in her life, even though I knew full well that she was in for some hormonally tumultuous years before she matured into whatever she would become—maybe a Rockette.

When I topped the crest of Nine Mile Hill outside Albuquerque, the setting sun at my back, the glittering city spread out below in the distance, I felt a little tightness in my throat. Being home for the holiday really was going to happen.

It was ten minutes to six when I walked into Ron and Victoria's snug bungalow. The scent of roasted turkey practically made my knees weak, and I spotted bowls of side dishes and two pecan pies on the kitchen counter. Drake and Freckles swooped in to bestow me with a pack-hug. Elsa, my beloved gram, was nibbling olives from the relish tray, and her caregiver, Dottie, was helping in the kitchen. I felt myself smiling at the rightness of it all.

Home. It felt good.

Author's Note

From the bottom of my heart, a huge wave of gratitude goes out to you—my readers. You bring joy to this writer. Once all the plotting and the words have come together, I always have some nervous moments when a new book is released. Judging by the initial reactions from editors and beta readers, it seems that pairing Charlie with the Heist Ladies was a big hit this time. I'm so glad. It was great fun writing them into scenes together, as well as letting each have her own moments in the action. A big shout-out to several fans who suggested doing this—you guys rock! I may just have to bring the Ladies together again at some point in the future. Stay tuned.

There's a bit of personal experience in this book. The character of Harvey, from the moment he walked out of his motel room door with a bowling bag for a suitcase, reminded me of my late father-in-law. And Harvey's incredible memory for every place he ever hunted or fished—well, that was my dad, into his ninety-fifth year. The road trip game "Saguaro!" was (as far as I know) invented by my husband, and every time we drive into southern Arizona, for the past twenty-some years, we each vie for being the first to spot them. One other guy gets a shout-out: the young man in a convenience store who treated me to a free Coke one afternoon. I'll never know your name, but your smile brought such a ray of sunshine into my day, at a time when I was dealing with so much frustration I was on the brink of tears. Thank you!

Another very important part of my real life that made it into this story is part about dog rescues in Mexico.

Barb's Dog Rescue outside Puerto Peñasco is the BEST! We adopted our sweet Daisy there nine years ago, and she's been an absolute blessing in our lives. We continue to financially support their work in whatever small ways we can. Barb and her team have rescued thousands of dogs from terrible situations and placed them in loving homes. You can sign up for their emails and learn more about the amazing work they do by visiting

https://www.barbsdogrescue.org/

And, as always, a huge thanks goes out to my editor, Stephanie Dewey, and my beta reader team: Marcia Koopmann, Susan Gross, Sandra Anderson, Isobel Tamney, and Paula Webb. Every book benefits from your expertise and sharp eyes on my manuscripts. Thank you, thank you, thank you!!

Connie Shelton is the *USA Today* bestselling author of more than 45 novels and 3 non-fiction books. She taught writing for six years and was a contributor to *Chicken Soup for the Writer's Soul.* She and her husband live in New Mexico with their dogs.

Sign up for Connie Shelton's free mystery newsletter at www.connieshelton.com and receive advance information about new books, along with a chance at prizes, discounts and other mystery news!

Contact by email: connie@connieshelton.com Follow Connie Shelton on Twitter, Pinterest and Facebook